JOHNNY CARELESS

JOHNNY CARELESS

A NOVEL

Kevin Wade

CELADON
BOOKS

NEW YORK

JOHNNY CARELESS. Copyright © 2024 by Back East Pictures, Inc. All rights reserved. Printed in the United States of America. For information, address Celadon Books, a division of Macmillan Publishers, 120 Broadway, New York, NY 10271.

www.celadonbooks.com

Library of Congress Cataloging-in-Publication Data

Names: Wade, Kevin, author.
Title: Johnny careless / Kevin Wade.
Description: First edition. | New York : Celadon Books, 2025.
Identifiers: LCCN 2024024591 | ISBN 9781250355102 (hardcover) |
    ISBN 9781250355119 (ebook)
Subjects: LCGFT: Thrillers (Fiction) | Detective and mystery fiction. | Novels.
Classification: LCC PS3573.A334 J64 2025 | DDC 813/.54—dc23/eng/20240604
LC record available at https://lccn.loc.gov/2024024591

Our books may be purchased in bulk for promotional, educational, or
business use. Please contact your local bookseller or the Macmillan Corporate
and Premium Sales Department at 1-800-221-7945, extension 5442, or
by email at MacmillanSpecialMarkets@macmillan.com.

First Edition: 2025

10 9 8 7 6 5 4 3 2 1

For Sasha

JOHNNY CARELESS

Chapter One

That early on a Sunday morning the beaches in Bayville were owned by the shorebirds grazing at the tidal buffet. It seemed to Police Chief Jeep Mullane that they were angry at the intrusion as the officers on scene taped off the perimeter and the EMTs carefully slid the body out of the water. The gulls screeched like snooty old ladies clutching their pearls and an osprey eyed the bald pink scalp of one EMT like it was a slice of deli ham. Jeep Mullane liked to challenge his days that way, the voice in his head looking to lighten up the grim times or jazz up the tedious ones. He'd learned the mind game from his father, an NYPD detective who loved classic cartoons. His dad would've described the osprey as having a napkin tied around its neck like a bib and with a knife and fork clutched in its talons. He liked to say, "Picture the wildlife as people and the people as wildlife. It helps sometimes."

Corporal Jackson was a couple steps ahead of Jeep as they headed to the waterline.

"Current's moving east so the Vollies are checking the shoreline going west looking for a vehicle and clothes, and they know not to touch anything," she said.

The local Volunteer Fire Department's calls largely came from a limited menu consisting of faulty smoke alarms, microwave fires, and seniors who'd fallen and couldn't get up. A body washing up on the beach would make for a welcome break, and if Jeep was being honest, that went for him, too.

"Slow down, Jackson. Walking in sand sucks for my knee, and you going ahead of me is not a good look."

Corporal Jackson slowed, winced and shrugged an apology.

"Copy that, Chief."

Jeep accelerated with a rolling gait to cover for his slight limp.

"C'mon, Jackson, try to keep up."

She laughed, as he'd intended.

The second squad of the Nassau County PD and their Field Medical Examiner were approaching the scene from the public beach parking lot. Jeep gritted his teeth and broke into a trot. He was Chief here and he was going to plant his flag first.

"What do we got?"

Sergeant Bondurant lifted the yellow tape and Jeep ducked under.

"In his skivvies so probably a night swim and looks like a boat or a Jet Ski hit him square in the kisser."

Jeep stepped around Bondurant and walked to the body. Male, white, turning to dappled shades of blue. Late thirties or forty, just shy of six feet, athletic build, with a full head of hair slicked back from the raw red mulch where his face used to be. One ear dangled, torn half off.

Jeep took a breath and held it, determined to keep down the breakfast burrito trying to claw its way back out.

The EMT flicked a strip of seaweed off the corpse's right ankle, looked closer.

"Got a tat here, Chief," he said, turning the ankle a few degrees out for a better look. "'X' marks the spot."

Jeep leaned over. Just above the anklebone, an inch or so square, a tattooed "X" in green ink, the borders blurred by the years.

Jeep stood up straight, sucked down another deep breath, and positively ID'd the deceased. But just to himself.

Twenty-One Years Earlier

John "Johnny" Payson Chambliss had a guy for everything, even at seventeen years old. Johnny had a guy for eleventh-hour exam cramming, for the mechanics of every sport he took up, for exotic strains of weed and CIA-grade fake IDs; Johnny had a fixer or a pro or an inside man for almost everything he was expected to excel at or avoid charges for, and they all traveled to him.

Except for tattoos; we had to travel for those. Dude called himself the Wizard of Ink and he operated from the curtained-off back room of a vintage vinyl records shop in Sea Cliff, a couple towns over. The Wizard didn't usually have office hours at ten on a Sunday night but Johnny had a guy for that, too.

That summer Johnny and me were like the pre-fallout Michael Jordan and Scottie Pippen of our elite-league lacrosse team. We'd spent the previous two months setting the nets on fire up and down Long Island, over to Westchester and up to southwest Connecticut. We took turns scoring at will, the two-man Four Horsemen of the Long Island Cannons, and we made the *Newsday* sports section for six Sundays running. After back-to-back blowouts that weekend we were headed to the championship rounds in Maryland.

It was my idea to up the stakes with matching tattoos; two crossed lacrosse sticks just above our ankles. If we won, the tats would be permanent symbols of our epic run, but if we didn't, they'd just forever brand us as losers. So we'd better fucking win.

We were walking back to our cars when Johnny broke the news.

He said, "Here's the thing. I can't go to Maryland."

I waited for the punch line, but Johnny just bent down and fiddled with the bandage over his tattoo.

"Seriously?"

"Dead serious," Johnny said.

"What the fuck?"

"I know. It sucks."

"You wanna tell me why?"

He stood back up and shrugged. "It's a family thing."

"Bailing on your team is a *family* thing?"

"I've got to go skiing in Portillo. We fly early Tuesday. It's a way-back tradition in my family, to ski in all four seasons. But my grandfather kinda made it into law before he croaked. Until you're twenty-five or married, whichever comes first, you gotta ski in all four seasons or your trust gets cut by a lot. A *lot* a lot. Supposed to teach us that upholding traditions requires effort and sacrifice or some bullshit."

I had no idea what to say because I could hardly understand the alibi. All I did was blink, like I wore glasses and had lost them.

"I didn't think we had a chance in hell of making the playoffs. But here we are. And I can't move the trip and I can't miss it."

After a moment I managed, "What the fuck is Portillo?"

"It's this mountain resort in Chile. It's where the Olympic skiers train in the summer."

He finally stood up and looked at me with an expression like he had wisdom it pained him to share.

"Thing is, it's good for *you*."

"How?"

"College scouts recruiting. You'll shine all the more if I'm not there."

"We'll get bounced in the second round if you're not there," I shot back.

"Scouts don't give a shit who wins. They're looking at individual players, not the teams. I'm set for college, but you—you could use a ride." He sounded certain.

It felt like an insult, when he put it like that. "Hey, fuck you, man."

"Jesus Christ, Jeep. Your old man's a New York City cop. That's a great thing but it's a low-paying thing. If you get a break out of Maryland, he'll get a break on your college nut. Win-win."

I walked to my car, a beater Subaru Forester, my mom's. Johnny buttoned the key fob and chirped the lock open on an Audi TT, all his.

"Coach know?"

"I kinda chickened out of telling him. Making an Irish exit."

I was way too sore and confused to be anywhere near coherent. I slid him a sharp "Happy trails, man," and got in my car and drove away with him yelling my name.

I felt it fell to me to tell Coach, so the next morning I called the Ace Hardware he part-timed at and he met me outside. When I gave him the news he didn't say anything at first, just looked away and made a couple noises. After a bit he looked back at me and screwed on a smile and shook his head.

"Lot of us took turns coaching Johnny Chambliss. Soccer, hockey, lax, since he was seven, eight. We nicknamed his ass a long time ago. He's Johnny Careless. He could care less, the wake he leaves just walking around."

As shitty a thing as Johnny did, it seemed wrong to me for the adults to brand you for how you were when you were seven or eight. And I liked Coach but I knew that his rep for being a "no-nonsense, hard-charging" guy also translated as "intolerant asshole" on the given day.

"He doesn't have a choice. I get the feeling there's a lot of, you know, apron strings, his family. Apron *chains*, more like it."

Coach pretended to weigh my point and chucked me on the shoulder, like we were in something together.

"What he *is*, if I'm being nice? He's from a different tribe than you and me, different customs, different standards. If you think they're your friends, keep your head on a swivel."

He walked back inside with a tossed-off "See you on the bus."

The Cannons got bounced in the second round, but I got 30 percent off to commit to Hamilton College, so Johnny and I were both right. But so was Coach, in ways that I didn't see coming no matter how fast my head could swivel.

Chapter Two

By 8:30 that morning there were two more taped-off perimeters; one around an early-nineties Land Rover Defender sitting under a stand of locusts by the kayak rack at the Lattingtown beach and the other around a bundle of clothes and a pair of penny loafers crammed in a crag in the rock jetty at the mouth of Beaver Creek a hundred yards west. The car's tags ran as registered to John Chambliss; the pants served up his wallet, with driver's license and business cards, and his Apple phone.

Local and county uniforms spanned out along the beach like old men scanning for coins.

Off by a picnic table, Detective Ron Arbogast of the Nassau County PD pocketed his cell phone and checked his watch. Arbogast looked to be in his midfifties, with a walnut tan and the kind of precise cop haircut that needed weekly attention. He strolled toward Jeep like a politician to a podium warming up to give his Lay of the Land Address. His young partner, Detective Ben Slocum, trailed behind like a loyal beagle.

"First off, we're gonna ask you and your team to set up a media staging area at site A. Press is piling up fast," Arbogast said.

"Copy that. Who we got?"

"So far News 12 and *Newsday*, local CBS and ABC, and stringers for the *Post* and the *News*. But the real question is, how do they know? I thought your calls went out encrypted."

The last delivered with a little editorial bent Jeep caught a whiff of.

"The calls do go out encrypted, but the Volunteer FDs get them straight up. And we got all vollies up here, and they all got somebody making a little something on the side feeding the juicy stuff to the press 'cause, you know, free country."

Arbogast slid him a sour look.

"Maybe want to get a handle on that," he said.

"We're trying, but limited budgets and all," Jeep said.

Arbogast said, "As of now we're treating it as an investigative DOA. You guys set up the media tent and we'll handle the rest."

Jeep took a deep breath.

"Copy?" Arbogast said.

Jeep weighed his protocol options and opted for collegial with a side of savvy.

"Sounds almost right."

"Almost?"

"It were me, and I know it's not, but it were me? That Land Rover isn't parked in the lot. It's *hidden*, just off it. And the owner forgot to lock it, and not for nothing, that's an Arkonik restoration of a vintage Defender ninety, trades for north of two hundred grand. Mr. Chambliss was likely on private business, likely distracted, likely had more on his mind than a midnight swim."

Arbogast gave him some side-eye. Slocum looked vaguely alarmed, like he didn't know correcting Arbogast was an option.

"That's a lot of takeaway off an unlocked vehicle," Arbogast said.

"Plus the body had a vivid tan line on its left wrist where a watch would be. Guy spends a couple hundred grand resto-modding a thirty-year-old truck generally wears a nice watch. The body wasn't wearing a nice watch and it isn't with his stuff. Just saying . . ."

"Just saying *what*, exactly?"

"It were me, I'd say 'investigative DOA' in public but procedurally I'd be leaning the other way."

"Gee, let me write this all down."

Slocum got out his notebook. Arbogast slid him a look, and he immediately put it away. Jeep pivoted.

"I'd like to make notification to the next of kin, with your consent."

"That's my role, as investigating detective," Arbogast said. "Well, mine or Detective Slocum's," he added generously.

"By chain of command protocols, a hundred percent," Jeep said. "But, Detectives, I grew up around here. I've known the vic's parents for almost twenty-five years. His ex-wife, too. The vic was my best friend for some of that time and a presence in my life for all of it."

Jeep hitched up his right pants leg and slid his sock down, exposing a small tattoo of two lacrosse sticks in an "X," the borders blurred by the years.

"Matching pair with the vic. Got 'em the summer we were seventeen. And I hope to God you're right about 'accident.' Me calling him 'vic' probably just me trying to sharpen my senses in case you find otherwise. I want to be of service here. And not for nothing, he always wore a watch. Mostly vintage and always valuable."

They regarded each other for a moment, Jeep trying for earnest and Arbogast trying for hard-ass and Slocum trying for neutral and all falling a little short.

"Anything we need to know . . ." Arbogast let the cue hang.

"You'll be the first," Jeep said. "Really appreciate the courtesy, Detectives."

Chapter Three

The Chambliss family had been headquartered on the North Shore of Long Island for four generations, with a money tree orchard on Wall Street and seasonal outposts in Vermont to the north and Jupiter Island to the south.

Jeep had sent Corporal Jackson to collect Pete Chambliss off the golf course at the Two Trees Club, where he had a standing tee time for twenty minutes after the 7:30 services at St. Luke's Episcopal ended. Jeep had called Niven Croft himself, figuring an ex-wife without a successor in the role also counted as next of kin but mostly because she'd been the third sector of their particular galaxy for most of their lives. He'd had her cell phone number in his contacts since they were teenagers. Everything changes in life except for the Verizon mobile number you got at twelve or thirteen. At least, around there.

She'd picked up on the fifth ring, her voice low and scratchy.

"It's nine o'clock on a Sunday morning so I hope you have a warrant."

She was, as always, quick and sharp and slightly intimidating. Jeep couldn't play that day.

"Are you at your parents' or in the city?"

"My parents', why?"

"Then I need you to meet me at the Chamblisses' soon as you can. I can't talk now, so don't call back, just get dressed and drive."

Johnny grew up in a vast Delano & Aldrich brick pile set on ten acres of hilltop in Mill Neck, where you could look out over the Sound and Oyster Bay and look down on the rest of the world. The long pea-gravel drive was immaculately raked, as always, and Jeep drove up it at five miles per hour so as not to disturb it, as always, and parked his vehicle by the tennis court pavilion and got out.

He stood still as time collapsed around him and the comings and goings of his younger self at this place bounced around in his head like cuts from a greatest hits album.

Jeep struck out at the front and kitchen doors and went around back and saw Gwen Chambliss before she saw him.

In her midsixties, she was more beautiful and elegant in her oxford shirt, khaki shorts and dusty Blundstones than most women were on their first wedding day. She was crouched over, tending to a bed of roses along the patio border. She barked at a speaker on the low wall.

"Alexa, play Warren Zevon."

The speaker obeyed in her polite voice and "Werewolves of London" came on.

Finally summoning the nerve, Jeep called out, "Mrs. Chambliss, good morning!"

She shielded her eyes from the sun as she looked his way.

"Gerald?"

Jeep's given name was Gerald Paul, initials "GP." His father had combined them to "Jeep" just after young Gerald started walking, for the way he always took the long way from point A to B by going over or under whatever obstacles could be utilized. Gwen Chambliss thought it was demeaning to Jeep and said so and never bought in.

"I'm afraid Johnny's not here."

"I came to see you, Mrs. Chambliss."

"Well aren't you sweet, and for God's sakes, it's Gwen!"

"Then you'd have to start calling me 'Jeep,' Mrs. Chambliss."

"Never!" she cried, throwing a hand in the air and laughing. "So how was the reunion?"

The local private day school, Shelter Rock Academy, had held its twentieth Upper School reunion the night before at The Mansion, an old estate turned conference-and-wedding venue in Glen Cove. Johnny had been expelled from two of the family's go-to New England prep schools and ended up graduating from Shelter Rock.

"Well, I went to Locust Valley public, so . . ."

She fanned a *silly me* gesture.

"I've known you so long I always think you must've been at Shelter."

Warren Zevon growled, "I'd like to meet his tailor." Jeep started to feel like this particular warm bath would actually make it harder to rip off the Band-Aid.

"Sorry, would you mind turning off the music?"

She stiffened and addressed the speaker as if it should've heard the first time.

"Alexa, off!"

The music died. She took a couple of steps toward Jeep.

"Is my husband going to be okay?"

Of course that's where she'd go, thought Jeep.

"Pete's fine. He's on his way."

Jeep inspected the tips of his shoes for a moment, looked up and met her gaze.

"It's Johnny. His body was found washed up on the beach in Bayville."

Jeep just tensed and froze, as if steeling himself to absorb a blast, as Pete Chambliss rounded the corner of the house double-time with a nine iron still in hand.

He clocked that Gwen was alive and well and looked to Jeep.

"The hell did he do now?"

"Johnny's dead, Pete. Johnny's dead," Gwen said. Her voice flat, going into shock.

Pete sagged with a shudder, like a big game animal taking the first bullet. He went to his wife and took her in his arms. Jeep arced around to the far side of the vast brick patio, invisible. There would be a hundred questions he couldn't answer but his job was to wait and placate them until Pete and Gwen were exhausted by the sudden-onset grief. Jeep sat in a wicker chair and fought the urge to fold in on his own feelings of shock and loss. There would be plenty of time, way too much time probably, to wrestle with that later. He had a job to do, one of those ones you really need to get right the first time.

He checked his phone, which had been buzzing since he'd arrived. He'd alerted his officers that he'd be off the radio while he made the notification. He had four missed calls from Corporal Jackson, five from Sergeant Bondurant, and a text from Bondurant that read: Mayor Donahue's house hit. Am on scene. Jeep typed in reply: Soon as I can. Still at Chambliss home.

He heard Niven calling out from inside the house, "Jeep? Johnny?"

"Out back," he replied, and got to his feet.

She came fast through the sunroom and the French doors and into the light. She took in Gwen and Pete still locked in their devastated embrace out on the lawn. She faced off with Jeep from ten feet away.

"Where's Johnny?"

"Johnny's gone," Jeep said.

"Gone where?" she said, like she was challenging him.

"His body was found washed up on the beach in Bayville earlier this morning."

"But I just saw him last night," she said.

Which always threw Jeep a little, the shock logic that assumes recent personal contact with someone means that he or she will still be walking the earth a short while later. Niven seemed to wobble.

"What happened?"

"Looks like he went swimming and got hit by a boat."

"Looks like?"

"Yes. It's early stages, so . . ."

Jeep broke off, staying out of the weeds.

Niven just stared at him for a moment, then summoned some steel.

"What do you think caught up with him?"

"I'm not thinking that way."

"Bullshit."

Jeep kept his mouth shut and opened his arms. She walked into him and laid her damp hair on his chest, and he put his arms around her as she heaved a sob.

Twenty Years Earlier

By 2:00 A.M. on Sunday mornings in June, the Adonis Diner on Jericho Turnpike was packed with high school seniors ending another Saturday night victory lap before their impending graduations. The crowd was Lawn Guyland diverse: pale male-rapper wannabes from Hicksville and Mineola; boisterous jocks from Chaminade and Saint Anthony's; packs of spray-tanned girlfriends from Roslyn and New Hyde Park helping their most molly-damaged sisters in and out of the ladies' room, shrieking laughs. The pre-game festivities started in a hundred different backyards and finished basements, but the post-game always ended up in a diner like this one, where I sat in a booth with Johnny and Niven. We'd come here from a dinner-dance at Two Trees so he and I were in blazers and khakis and she in a slip dress that had broadcast her nipples at attention all night. My date had begged off but Niven was a machine. It was Johnny's turn to order.

"Two scrambled, well-done corned beef hash—"

The waitress cut him off. "We're out of the hash."

"How can you be out of the hash? You're famous for the homemade hash."

"Maybe that's why we're out of it," she said. "Plus, you know, it's two in the morning."

"Yeah, two in the morning at a place that advertises everywhere how good their homemade corned beef hash is in hopes that people go way out of their way for it."

"Sonny, I don't got all night."

"I'm not your son."

"Thank God for small favors," she said.

Johnny got that look he'd get when he felt someone was poking at him for being born him. He was handsome, all right, but he could act like he knew it. When Coach was grousing once about some shit Johnny pulled, he said to me that Johnny had "a very punchable face."

"Tell you what, Miss Trunchbull. Have the cook open a can of Hormel's, smash it on the griddle 'til it's crusty—"

She cut him off, clearly pissed off now. "We don't have the canned stuff, just the homemade."

"Except when you don't?"

Niven got in his face.

"You're not Jack Nicholson and we're not in *Five Easy Pieces*. Just fucking order something."

She did Nicholson's flat drawl damn well. Johnny had recently discovered the early Nicholson films and made us watch them with him, some twice.

Johnny slumped a little, as close to embarrassed as a guy like him got.

"Cheeseburger deluxe, medium, and a vanilla Coke."

She walked off. Johnny called after her, "Which I could've ordered anywhere!"

After we finished eating, Johnny picked up the check the waitress had slapped on the table and said the meal was on him and sorry for making a scene.

He ordered a coffee to go at the counter as he waited in line for the cashier. Niven asked me to wait with her in the parking lot while she smoked a cigarette.

Johnny came out a couple minutes later and tossed the coffee cup in the bushes and held up a green slip.

"Breakfast was on Miss Trunchbull," he said.

I grabbed the slip and checked it. It was for fifty-three dollars and change.

"What'd you do?" I said.

"Got a check for the coffee and just paid that one is what I did."

"But not the food?" Niven asked.

"Why?" I asked.

Johnny said, "'Cause you can't treat people like that and then expect them to pay full freight. Matter of principle."

"Jesus, let's get out of here," Niven said.

She tossed her cigarette and headed for Johnny's car.

"Be good," Johnny said to me with a bear hug. "Talk in the P.M." He took off after her.

I stood there until they'd pulled out of the lot and then I walked back inside. The waitress was in the ear of the fat guy working the register. She pointed at me, all indignant, and said, "That's one of them."

I had the check in hand and my wallet out. I was flush with cash from caddying two loops that day. I peeled off three twenties and handed them to the fat man.

"My friend got mixed up with the checks."

The waitress sneered, "Bull*shit*. Your friend skated."

"I just paid. Keep the change. End of story."

The fat man sized up my khakis-and-blazer look. He spoke with a heavy Greek accent.

"I believe my niece. I believe he skated but you chickened out and came back in. I got that right, Richie Rich?"

My chicken parm had been gloppy and barely lukewarm and my

mellow weed-and-Budweiser buzz had turned into a splitting headache. In a usual mood I would've flashed my dad's Benevolent Association courtesy card and pointed out I was a cop's kid from Bayville and not some Richie Rich, but instead I said, "Sorry, did you say she's your *niece* or your *piece*?"

I was too busy patting myself on the back to fend off his punch. It was hard and fast and I went down the same way.

Chapter Four

Walter Donahue was the mayor of Centre Brookville and so was one of Jeep's five bosses, along with the mayors of Matinecock, Lattingtown, Mill Neck and Bayville. While the other mayors looked on their positions as the spare-time noblesse oblige gigs they in fact were, Mayor Donahue was very proud and, in his words, "extremely proactive." He'd even floated the campaign slogan MAKE CENTRE BROOKVILLE GREAT AGAIN, but it got shot down by his inner circle as both derivative and a little chewy.

He was resting his hams against the hood of the built-in Viking eight-burner BBQ on the back patio of his vast McMansion and he was in no mood for Jeep's recap of the bleeding-heart bail reforms that handcuffed cops instead of criminals. His new Porsche 911 had been stolen from his driveway the night before and that was all that mattered.

"The fuck?" he said. "Then what am I paying you for, Mullane?"

It was the fourth or fifth time he'd called Jeep by his last name like it rhymed with "dumbass." Jeep was grateful the mayor had at least asked him outside and away from his officers.

"You're paying me to identify and apprehend the perpetrators. Which I am in the process of doing."

"Gee, don't break a sweat."

Any other morning, water off a duck's back. But on that morning, fresh from the shock of Johnny's death and the Chamblisses' pain and grief, Jeep barely kept a grip.

"The surveillance footage from your system shows what we already knew. This was an opportunistic hit by a highly skilled, well-organized syndicate that has been preying on the North Shore from Great Neck out to Cold Spring Harbor."

Since the early spring a crew of undocumented immigrants had been targeting those suburbs with skills and smarts that were extraordinary, especially for a ragtag bunch whose median age appeared to be eighteen. The surveillance footage showed a likely stolen Audi S6 pulling up, two males popping out in hoodies and Covid masks, and then departing within sixty seconds with the mayor's Porsche. Jeep wondered if the driver used a stopwatch and gave out attaboys at the post-game debriefing.

"Opportunistic, how?"

"Shopped at the Americana recently?" The Americana was a high-end mall in Manhasset where the parking lot could look like a Porsche/Ferrari/Bentley Cars & Coffee meet.

"Thursday," Donahue said.

"They probably tailed you home."

"But the house was locked and the alarms were armed."

"My guess is they clocked the number on your mailbox, doubled it, and entered it on the separate keypad for the garage doors. Is the code one-six-one-six?"

"Fuck me," Donahue said, after a moment.

"The only good news, if you could call it that, is that if you or Mrs. Donahue had heard and confronted them, they would've just fled empty-handed."

"How's that good news?"

"They haven't killed or injured anyone in the commission of these crimes. Or even entered a house. At least, as of yet."

He puffed up his cheeks and blew out.

"That car was Paint to Sample. Waited more than two years for it."

"And they probably unloaded it in two hours."

"Where?"

"Port of Newark," I said.

"Well, it's an Irish Green Targa 4S. It kind of sticks out, you know? Can't they canvass the port or whatever you call it?"

"You're right, a car like that would stick out. My guess would be it was loaded straight into a waiting container, then into the cargo hold of a ship that left port already."

If Donahue's look bordered on contempt, the border was pretty unsecured.

"You've got an answer for everything, don't you, Mullane."

"No sir, I wish I did. And please, call me by my first name. It's *Chief* Mullane."

Jeep pulled into his driveway just after nine thirty with a boxed pizza and his laptop on the seat next to him. His stomach was churning from the high tide of black coffee and bad news. The Mercedes G-Wagen surprising him by the brick front walk flew the flags of a particular tribe of the North Shore: parking stickers on the rear bumper for two golf clubs, a yacht club and a winter sports club, and rear-glass decals spelling out Tulane and Dartmouth. Jeep figured it was Niven's mother's car and that the day was about to get even longer. He grabbed a slice of pizza from the box, bit off half of it, and went around back.

Niven was sitting in one of the twin Adirondack chairs by the bulkhead overlooking the beach and the Long Island Sound from his backyard. He'd bought the house from his mother after his father had passed and she'd decided to move near her sisters in Sarasota.

"Hey," he said, and she turned to him.

"So pretty here."

"Yeah, it works," he said.

"What's it like, living in the house you grew up in? We never really talked about it."

Because Jeep was more than a little self-conscious about it. Because moving back to your hometown was a pretty small-town move. But moving into the actual house you grew up in maybe won you a dubious distinction, loser-wise.

"Well, I got a break on the price, and I changed enough so that it feels like mine. Plus, you know, my father didn't beat me and my mother wasn't a drunk, so no, like, traumatic memories or anything."

He sat down in the chair next to hers and wolfed down the crust.

"It's been a long day."

"What's that supposed to mean?" she said.

"Is there something you need?" he said.

"It's been a long day for everybody. Except Johnny. He had a short day." She slid a frown at him.

"You're right, point taken. Forgive me."

She looked at him like gauging his sincerity. She found it adequate, apparently.

"We're good."

She stood up, stretched, arching her back. "The Nassau County detectives got the contacts list from the reunion last night and called everybody and we have to all go in for interviews tomorrow."

"Standard procedure," he said. "Did you talk to Johnny before he left? Was he meeting someone, did he say?"

"I talked to him on and off all night. We kept mixing in and out the whole time. And no, not that he told me."

She looked away. Jeep waited for more.

"He in a beef with anybody at the thing?"

"No."

"So, nothing you want to share?"

"*Share?* Is that how cops talk now?" Only half kidding.

"I'm off duty, you and I are friends. And not for nothing, and not like you did, but I lost him, too."

"Point taken." She held out a hand. "There's a vigil down near where they found him. I came here to get you."

Jeep tried to read her in the dark. He had a hundred questions for her but kept it zipped out of respect and chivalry for the ex-wife, the day after the night of.

"So's I can squash the summons for the bonfire they set?"

Getting a smile, as intended. "Exactly," she said, then she flashed him a look that meant business.

"It's your reunion, too. You grew up with practically everybody. And you were The Rock, and now you're Chief Rock, and everybody wants you there and needs you there."

Jeep held her look for a moment, ducked a nod, and stood up.

"Give me a minute to change." He started toward the house.

Forty or so alumni of the Shelter Rock Academy Class of 2003 were milling around a bonfire on the beach as a Bluetooth speaker blasted the White Stripes' "Seven Nation Army," a favorite of Johnny's from back in those days. Jeep got a beer from a cooler and made the rounds of old rec leagues and Cannons Lacrosse teammates, a few girls now women he'd dated or hooked up with and a few who'd laughed him off and one who he'd fallen hard for and who said she loved him back but turned out was just using him to piss off her parents after they forced her "debut" at a black-tie ball in New York. He did pretty well with the names of some friendlies and frenemies he hadn't seen in twenty years and eventually found himself alone at the water's edge listening to a guy he couldn't remember give a rambling toast to "our brother behind the sun."

If, like Niven said, they wanted him there and needed him there, they were as good as ever at hiding it. He felt like he'd felt at gatherings with this crowd twenty years ago; like after twenty seconds or so whoever Jeep talked to glanced over Jeep's shoulder in search of a more strategic option.

Niven walked up with a red go-cup spilling white wine and leaned her back against him.

"A word of advice?" he said. "Don't try to hide anything from the detectives tomorrow. They *will* know if you are."

"I'm not hiding anything," she said.

"You're always hiding something, including right now. And a half-decent detective can make Jesus himself think twice did he rob the 7-Eleven."

"I didn't rob a 7-Eleven."

"It's an exaggeration, like to make a point."

"I got that," she said, shutting it down.

She clenched the lip of her cup in a bite, reached for his hands and crossed them around her middle, and it occurred to Jeep that maybe it wasn't them that needed him there but her.

Eighteen Years Earlier

On Long Island's North Shore, as it is in many suburbs, your destination the night before Thanksgiving was set in stone. Everyone home on break from college arrived by nine at the designated local bar to brag, flirt, lie, laugh, console, get even, and most important, get hammered with the kids you grew up with. In our zip code, in that time, the bar was the Beagle's Nest, where we'd all had our first legal hometown cocktails. It was near the train station in Locust Valley and had the additional advantage of a back patio for overflow and a pocket park bandstand out back from there for the overflow from the overflow. Johnny's guy at Beagle's was the owner's son, so we had the prime booth across from the bar and closest to the door. We could say hello to everybody without moving an ass cheek or spilling a drop.

Johnny and Niven had been together for four years by then and were still going strong, despite her being at Dartmouth in New Hampshire and him being at Georgetown in D.C. and the miscommunications and temptations that that geography can bring. My plus-one was Elise, another in a line of trust-funded NESCAC girls who fell for my salt-of-the-earth, Timberlands-and-cargo-shorts, pickup-driving Lax-Bro charms. As I remember, Elise dumped me just before Christmas when she got bored with my act and took up some Todd's offer of Round Hill in Jamaica.

Johnny and Niven made such a great couple that older siblings and even some parents had started weighing in on whether or not they'd get married right after graduation and whether or not that union would end up as a "mulligan," destined to end within a few years, thus predicting that a second, "do-over," marriage was in the cards for both of them.

Johnny had his arm around Niven, both of them slumping in the booth, pretty drunk. Johnny slipped a hand down her sweater; she was fine with that. So Johnny being Johnny must've tweaked a nipple, the way she erupted and threw an elbow at his ear. They wrestled some, knocked over Elise's Southside, and then calmed down. He told her he loved her in a voice that cracked her up.

The woman who walked in around eleven clearly wasn't from here. She was stunningly beautiful; glowing copper-brown skin and green eyes and hair like a lion's mane that went halfway down her back. She wore a suede trucker jacket way too light for late November and tight jeans tucked into tooled cowboy boots. She scanned the room and landed on Johnny and just stayed pinned on him, like waiting for the heat from her stare to set his shirt on fire and get his attention. He was busy one-upping some Club mate so I gave him a kick under the table and jerked my head in her direction.

Johnny, like he'd seen a ghost, mumbled, "Gotta 'scuse me a minute," and bolted from the booth and got her out the door.

Niven didn't see a thing. She was all wrapped up looking at selfies from Portugal on Elise's cell phone.

By last call Johnny was still gone, calls and texts had gone unanswered, and Niven was about as drunk as you can get and still keep your eyes open.

Elise and I poured her into my pickup and propped her up between us and drove her to her parents' house in Brookville.

We got her out and both took an armpit and Niven spoke for the first time in like forty minutes, jerking her arm from Elise.

"I don't want her!"

Elise gingerly handed her half of Niven over to me and I danced her to the door and tried for a soft landing to the night.

"Fucking Johnny, huh?"

"What about him?" she said, suddenly sharper.

"Well I mean, just taking off like that," I said.

"I'm sure he's got his reasons. And I'm sure he doesn't need you for his lawyer."

"I wasn't. What the fuck?"

"Can I do you a favor, Jeep? I'd like to do you a favor. Jump you over like, ten puddles here."

I let her go and took a step back. She stiff-armed a pillar for support and looked at me with one eye half closed.

"Quit trying to get in. It's not gonna happen. You're a nice guy, you are, and you're cute too, and according to Khaki Stubblefield you go down there like it's your favorite flavor ice cream. But here's the thing? You're *from* here, yeah. But you're always gonna be signing the guest book, you're never gonna be a *member*."

I felt stung, burned, crushed, betrayed and sucker punched all at the same time. I rang the doorbell and hurried off down the walk as lights went on upstairs.

I ducked her calls all the next day, but Niven finally found me and demanded I talk to her. She said she didn't remember how she got home or anything about it. Her father knew my truck.

I wouldn't tell her what she'd said. I was afraid that if I did, it would cut my chances of ever being able to forget it.

She kept pressing and pressing and finally I told her that I'd gotten her to the door and that she'd looked me in the eye and said, "Feel how wet I am."

It took her a second and then she whacked me in the shoulder and started laughing her ass off and I went along.

I never saw the woman in the suede trucker jacket again but I did find out her name was Catalina and that she'd taken trains, planes and automobiles all the way from Chile to the North Shore of Long Island just to see Johnny.

Chapter Five

Jeep's Monday started much the same as his Sunday, not quite as early but arguably worse, coming off a night's sleep broken by alarmingly literal bad dreams. The wake-up call from Corporal Jackson had a milder tone, another Grand Theft Auto instead of another Corpse On Beach. He chugged some cold-brew coffee from the fridge and grabbed a slice of last night's pizza from the box and hit the road.

The Terhune residence was one of those low-slung glass-and-cedar jobs called mid-century modern but read to Jeep like Bond movie villain fortress. Beau Terhune paced his Belgian block driveway in whale-print shorts and a hedge fund–branded fleece vest and regarded Jeep like Jeep was a slow new intern at the firm.

"Of course they were locked," he said.

"And the keys were inside the house. Not tucked under a wheel well, say."

"Of course, inside. The bench in the mudroom, where we always put them."

He turned to the house and started walking. Jeep and Jackson filed after him, heading through the kitchen and into a "mud room" that was very roomy but not one bit muddy. Terhune rifled through a bowl on a pine workbench just inside, pawing through hair clips and junk mail and orphaned AA batteries. He came up empty.

He turned to Jeep with the slightest hitch in his command.

"They're gone."

He checked the knob on the door to the outside.

"Lily must have forgotten to lock up after she let Chester back in."

Jeep threw a glance at Jackson, who frowned quickly and shook her head just a little. The crew had entered the house. Which was new. Which was not good.

"What?" Terhune demanded.

Jeep tried for casual and mostly succeeded.

"They're smart. Experience tells them ninety-percent chance the keys are by the mudroom or kitchen door."

"Jesus. They come *inside*?"

"Only if it was unlocked and, you know, easy opportunity. And they're only after cars," Jeep said.

"You talk like you're so sure. But my wife was walking around down here in just her underwear. I mean, come *on*, man."

Corporal Jackson was a young Black woman who stood about five-five. Men like Beau Terhune barely gave her notice when she was with Jeep, even though she wore the same basic uniform. So they always got a little distracted when she did step in, not least because she talked so incredibly fast.

Jackson said, "Mr. Terhune, I get where you're coming from and I can feel your 'my taxpayer dollars at work' outrage that this could happen in your beautiful home but it is important to remember two things: (a) these guys are stealing cars for cash and they need to be in and out fast so they have zero bent for forcible sex on the job, and if one did, the others would bust his ass pronto, and (b) you need to lock and alarm your doors *always* 'cause it's a gorgeous house you've got here but the way you got it landscaped so sparsely your great good fortune is on display like a Macy's Christmas window for any lowlife who happens by."

All in, like, five seconds. Terhune looked a little rattled and managed, "Thanks for that, Officer."

"Anytime," Jackson said.

While Jackson finished taking the report, Jeep looked for Sergeant Bondurant down past the pool house at the western edge of the property.

"Bondi?" Jeep called out.

"Back here, boss," Bondi said from the other side of a thick stand of arborvitae and bramble. Jeep pushed through and it opened onto a two-track service road for the power-line towers that ran south to north. There was some flotsam of empty Red Bull cans and cigarette butts at their feet and three-point-turn tire tracks, which ran from that point heading south.

"Probably got on from one of the cul-de-sacs down toward the Expressway," Bondurant said. "Watched for the lights to go out and then got up to their dirty deeds."

Bondurant sometimes liked to talk as if they were lawmen in the Wild West. It got old fast, but he was a tireless cop and a good man.

Jeep walked a ten-foot circle around the detritus, looked up and down the service road. Smart, he thought. Come in from back here, avoid the license plate readers and stoplight cameras on the surface roads on the mapped route.

Jeep spotted a glint in the grass by the thicket. He bent over, looking at a burner phone.

"You got gloves and a bag?" he asked.

"'Course," Bondurant said.

Jeep pointed at the phone.

"Run this down to Sam Wong at Computer Crimes in Mineola and remind him he owes me a favor. I'll call in for a warrant for the extraction."

"There a wish list?"

Jeep said, "Texts and photos. The smoking guns, for a thing like this, is where they're taking pictures and what they're texting about with who."

The Centre Brookville Police Department headquarters was a U-shaped assemblage of three mobile office trailers off a dead-end lane shared with a bird sanctuary. The department had been split off from the larger Upper Brookville PD nine months earlier in some gerrymandering and one-upmanship among the mayors of the surrounding incorporated villages and was awaiting funding for a proper facility. Jeep was the very first Chief of the newly formed entity, and as he pulled into the lot and spotted Mayor Donahue waiting for him, he had second thoughts for the thousandth time about taking the job. Jeep parked and got out.

"Morning, Mayor Donahue." He liked to be called "mayor" or "sir" and it didn't cost Jeep anything to play along.

"You ever seen *Jaws*, Chief Mullane?"

"Yes, sir."

Who the hell hasn't, Jeep kept to himself.

"The mayor in *Jaws* was dead right taking the stand he did. His *job* was to protect and preserve the social and economic well-being of the community he'd been elected to serve. Now of course Hollywood's going to play a conservative like him for laughs and they did but the *fact is* he was some kind of hero in that movie."

"Hadn't thought of it that way, Mr. Mayor."

"I heard the Terhunes got hit last night. We've got a big problem here. We've got sharks on our beaches."

"And . . . we're gonna need a bigger boat?" Jeep regretted it the moment he said it.

"You think this is funny?"

"No sir, I think it's dead serious. But I don't know what it has to do with the movie *Jaws*."

"Illegals stealing cars right out of our homes equals sharks on our beaches. Threatens our personal safety, our way of life, and the value of those homes. Get it?"

Jeep just nodded.

"The Terhunes' is the, what, fifth car stolen this month?"

"Fifth and sixth, an Audi and a Range Rover," Jeep said.

"You know, Mullane, it occurs to me, and not just me, that we hire a big-city cop as our Chief of Police and all of a sudden we've got big-city crime going on here. Not a good look for you."

"All due respect, this is a wave cresting from Great Neck to—"

"I know that. I don't care about that. I care about *here*. And you should, too."

Jeep took a deep breath. Looked at his shoes and listened to his father. Looked back up at Donahue, square in the eye, showing nothing, saying nothing, "waiting the other guy out," like his old man said to do. It didn't take long with a guy like Donahue. Guys like Donahue took silence for surrender and as license to keep right on bulldozing the days.

"Get the sharks off our beaches!" he said, jabbing a finger in punctuation.

Donahue turned away and walked to his Porsche Gold Coast courtesy vehicle, got in and drove off.

At his desk in trailer three, Jeep rolled calls, checking in with his counterparts at the other North Shore PDs. Which meant he was addressed as, variously, Wrangler, El Grand Cherokee, Jeepster and Scout. Jeep always let slide that a Scout was actually an old International Harvester 4X4, being a good sport about the kidding.

Oyster Bay had had a quiet weekend but Glen Cove had three thefts, Jericho two, and Lloyd Harbor two. A couple of ambitious Great Neck cops chased a Bentley Bentayga to the Queens County line then had to turn back to get ripped a new one by their CO. It was pretty much a standing order among all the departments that you gave chase only if you had confirmation that a murder or serious injury had been committed in the commission of the crime. The risk of collateral damage to property and especially innocent bystanders was simply too great, even for a Bentley.

Bondurant knocked and entered at the same time. Jeep had given up pushing back as he'd yet to interrupt anything more vital than a desk lunch or a chair nap.

"Wong's got a full plate but he said you could stop by around noon tomorrow and he should have whatever he could get off the phone."

"Thanks, Bondi. Will do."

"And he said that now you owe him one."

"Nah, he never could keep score."

Jeep fully expected excuses when he reached out to Detective Slocum for an update on their investigation and was pleasantly surprised when Slocum invited him for a drink and a download after work. Jeep knew he had two strikes on him where Nassau PD was concerned; he was ex-NYPD, which they assumed gave him a big head and a big foot, plus now, as a small-town chief, they regarded him the way they thought the NYPD regarded them, as speed-trap jockeys and parade hounds. It was all based on false premises; there was in fact plenty of mutual respect and cooperation between the departments, but policing is a people business and everybody needs somebody they can dump on, so fuck the actual facts.

Jeep had changed into khakis and a blazer from his stash at the office and met Slocum in a booth at Thai Palace near the Second Precinct HQ on Jericho Turnpike.

"Appreciate you doing this," Jeep said, slipping into the booth.

"'You scratch my back, I scratch yours' always worked for me," Slocum said.

This seemed to Jeep like an off-key line, coming from a detective who couldn't be out of his twenties and who'd make a good undercover Mormon if the need arose.

"I haven't done much scratching. The press we were supposed to handle kinda disappeared as fast as they showed up. Nothing even in *Newsday*."

"Maybe it was a big news day at *Newsday*," Slocum said.

"No such thing on Long Island unless there's a hurricane coming or a politician getting perp-walked," Jeep said. "Somebody put some kind of word out?"

"How would they do that?" Slocum said. The question seemed to trip him up a little.

"You tell me. I'm still a rookie chief, there's a lot comes at me that used to be above my pay grade."

"Be way above my pay grade, if that's what's going on. But I don't have any intel that it is."

The waitress stopped by. Jeep ordered a tap IPA and Slocum a refill Bloody Mary.

"And a Dewar's and soda, hon," Detective Arbogast said, appearing behind her. He slid into the booth next to Slocum.

"Detective," Jeep said.

"Sorry I'm late, got waylaid with work," Arbogast said. "Slocum and I tag-teamed the interviews today and I had a couple loose ends."

Jeep just nodded. He'd noticed Arbogast alone at the bar on his way in. He wasn't late, he'd been waiting. Jeep was being tag-teamed himself.

"Your late friend Chambliss had a sealed criminal record. You know about that?" Arbogast said.

"Yes, I did. A bad choice from a long time ago."

Arbogast clocked him for a moment, not hiding it at all. And then he moved on.

"I'm pretty sure the ex-wife is hiding something."

Niven never listens, Jeep thought.

"Like?" Jeep said.

"I don't know. Just a feeling. But it's not like I can put her at the wheel of the boat that hit him, so . . ." He shrugged.

The old-school term for a Detective Arbogast was hairbag, from back in the NYPD day when a cop had to bring a bag of his hair to his CO to prove he got a haircut while on duty and wasn't just off eating or drinking or catching some z's. Jeep's old man used to say that if you gave that kind of cop a lie detector test and asked, "What do you do at your job?" the only answer that would pass would be "as little as possible." But Jeep showed respect and played along.

"She always acts like she's got a secret and it's always some bullshit thing only she'd think was important. Some kind of defense mechanism, I guess."

Arbogast laughed. "If I walked around looking like her all my life, I'd want some 'defense mechanisms,' too, I guess."

Arbogast threw Jeep a mild leer, like testing some waters. Jeep played it neutral.

"She's easy on the eyes, as the old guys say."

Arbogast squinted at "old guys" but let it go.

"This Chambliss was a real character, what I heard," Arbogast said.

"He was. He also *had* real character," Jeep said. Guys like Arbogast always made Jeep want to weigh in for whoever's rep a guy like Arbogast was stepping on.

Slocum did a little *duh-me* tap to his forehead.

"Chief, were *you* at the reunion?" he said.

"No, I went to the public school. Shelter Rock was for kids whose parents could afford boarding school but wanted the kids at home so they could keep tabs on them. It was also for kids who got bounced from boarding school and whose parents wanted to save face saying they missed them too much and wanted them close to home 'cause time goes so quickly blah blah blah."

Setting the two detectives at ease with his candor.

"And that'd be Chambliss?"

"Pretty much. The ex-wife, too. They spent junior and senior years at Shelter, not all four."

"So, you and him were friends from?" Arbogast said.

"Just you know, around. Got tight through Cannons Lacrosse in high school summers."

The waitress placed their drinks. Jeep took a long sip.

"So, what's the story?" Jeep said, looking from one to the other.

Slocum shrugged, Arbogast did a little dismissive thing with his hand that read *what story?*

Arbogast said, "The Marine Unit and the Coasties are canvassing, see if anyone thought they hit a log in the dark. Also looking at security footage from the marinas and yacht clubs, but there's not a lot of leisure traffic on the Sound that time of night and the night fishers we talked to didn't have dick. The ME put the time of death at about midnight, give or take. And he was hit by something, no salt water in the stomach, dead on impact."

"So, tragic accident," Jeep said.

"Walks like a duck . . ." Arbogast said, and took another swallow of scotch and soda.

Slocum said, "But the interviews, the people with him the night of? Pretty interesting, I gotta admit."

Jeep bit. "Interesting how?"

"Like how almost to a man and woman they all said they knew him. That he was cool to hang with, party, ski, get high with, do business with, or get fucked over doing business with, according to this one guy. Etcetera etcetera. A few seemed genuinely sad he'd died, a few threw him under every bus that came by. Some hadn't seen him in the twenty years, some were still regulars in the rotation, one married and divorced him. But here's the thing, except for the ex-wife? They all summed up with some version of 'I knew Johnny as much as anybody but nobody *knew* Johnny.'"

Jeep could see how that tribe could frame Johnny like that; even in early middle age they still measured their relationships by the specific calibrations of status and wealth and relative success they'd been schooled in, growing up around there. Johnny could seem to float above that on his cloud of seemingly effortless cool. You had to be watching for the times he fell off that cloud and hit the pavement. And open to accepting that his acts of kindness were just that. You had to actually give a shit, Jeep thought but did not share, especially with Arbogast present.

"But nothing gives off a whiff?" Jeep said.

"Nothing so far, no," Slocum said.

Arbogast added, "And if somebody did have that big a beef with him, this crowd? They don't get their hands dirty, their lawyers do."

Then Arbogast looked at Slocum like, *I got it from here*, and sat back, expansive.

"Jeep, may I call you Jeep?" Arbogast said.

"Sure."

"Now, I know it goes without saying, but I do wanna just shine a light on it. You're a smart guy, second-generation NYPD, so I'm not telling you anything you don't already know. But just for the record? You do know you've got to stay away from this thing, right?"

Jeep played dumb, just for fun.

"I do?"

Putting them both at unease, a little.

Arbogast said, "Well, yeah. It's County's case. It's *our* case. And you know from your days as a detective, you gotta hand off cases you got this kind of personal interest in. I don't need to tell you, that situation? You're looking for things that aren't there and missing the things that actually are."

"Makes sense. A good cop'd take himself right off it," Jeep said.

"And you are a good cop, Jeep. But I feel for you, an old friend, it must be tough to have to just step away," Arbogast said.

Jeep made like he appreciated the empathy.

"It is," he said. "But you're right, I knew the vic, we were buds, I could go off on detours looking for a better reason he's dead than just some fucked-up twist of fate."

"Only natural," Arbogast said. "But it is what it is."

Fifteen Years Earlier

I was riding shotgun, and Johnny was driving his new-old Porsche 911 west on Northern Boulevard past Oyster Bay Cove. Johnny had graduated from Georgetown the week before, after a five-year scenic route to a bachelor's degree. The car was his present from his father, a flawless black-on-black 1992 Carrera 4 that came with a windy lecture from Pete about how air-cooled 911s were the true 911s and how the company had betrayed its origins when they traded the beautiful music of the cooling fan for a radiator. It was one of those rich people distinctions I could barely follow but it seemed to me that the car was more like something Pete cared about but gave to Johnny in the hope it might become an enthusiasm they could share.

I looked over at the speedometer; he was doing 80 in a 50. "You know the cops love them some Friday night speed traps out here."

"This thing's like silk," Johnny said as he eased off and downshifted.

We'd been to a party in Cold Spring Harbor and he'd had a few pops but was nothing approaching friends-don't-let-friends-drive-drunk drunk. His mother's birthday present to him was the Warren Zevon CD playing through the upgraded Bose speakers. He turned up the volume as the next song came on and Warren Zevon started singing that he was staying at a Marriott with Jesus and John Wayne, Warren waiting for a chariot and the others for a train. Whatever that meant.

Johnny shouted over the music. "This is called 'My Ride's Here.' It's the prettiest song about kicking the bucket there ever was, you ask me."

I couldn't follow how that was the story, but the song did have a kind of urgency to it.

Johnny turned the volume down and looked over at me with an odd smile. "Do me a favor, and don't laugh?" he said.

"Okay," I said.

"If we're still friends when I kick the bucket, have them play this at my funeral."

"You got it, James Dean."

"I'm serious."

I looked over. He was. Maybe he'd had more than a couple pops, which was possible. Some nights the distance between fun Johnny and morbid Johnny was like, half a beer. But he seemed as focused and present as he was when stone-cold sober.

"Okay. Done and doner," I said.

"Let's take Mill River," he said.

Mill River Road was a curvy descent into the western edge of Oyster Bay and the road of choice in a car like that. Johnny started the song over and we just rode and listened.

Around a blind curve halfway down, a big buck ran across the road in front of us. Johnny whipped the wheel and hit the brakes but the rear end kept going and we ended up facing the other way in a ditch.

I was okay. He was okay. The Porsche, not so much. We got out and saw the left rear fender was crunched up against a rock and one back wheel was suspended over the drainage culvert by a couple feet.

"Fuck!" Johnny said. "Fuck fuck fuck fuck FUCK!"

A soccer mom in a Volvo wagon slowed and powered down her window.

"You boys okay?"

"Yeah fine thank you so much," Johnny said.

"I'll call nine-one-one for you but the sitter got sick so I gotta go," she offered up as she rolled off.

"You don't need to do that, ma'am, we're all good here!" Johnny shouted. She just kept going.

"FUCK!" he shouted.

I tried the back bumper. No way this was a two-man job.

"The cops will have a tow truck guy on call."

"I did some blow," Johnny said. "C'mere, look at my eyes."

He leaned over one of the headlights. "Look at my eyes."

I did. Pupils the size of pinheads.

"What the fuck, man," I said.

"Two little lines was all, just before we left, so sharp for the drive home."

"Real sharp," I said.

"They gonna shine a light in my eyes?"

"They might," I said.

"Fucking deer! We were golden 'til that fucking deer!"

I walked over and reached in to turn the engine off.

"Where's the ignition?"

"On the left," he said.

I found it, killed it.

"I was driving," I said.

"What do you mean?" Johnny said.

"All I had was a club soda. I'm taking a Z-Pak for a sinus thing and you're not supposed to drink. Plus, I've got courtesy cards for Nassau and Suffolk."

"What's a courtesy card?" Johnny said.

"Has my name and a detective's name and his cell number and says, 'Please extend all courtesies.' I get them from my dad."

"Like 'get out of jail free'?"

"Not quite, but all we need for this."

We could hear a siren in the distance.

"You'd do that for me?" Johnny said.

Looking at me like a grateful little kid, just for a moment. Then shaking it off, cool again.

Johnny said, "Get your prints all over the door handle and the wheel."

"They're not gonna dust the car," I said.

"Cops make me paranoid, case you hadn't noticed."

"Where's your phone?" I said.

"Driver's side door pocket."

I got it out and tossed it to him. The siren was drawing closer, you could see blue lights strobing the sky.

"We're good," I said.

That Sunday night Johnny's parents hosted a dinner in honor of Johnny's graduation in a private dining room at the Two Trees Club. Johnny's sister, Phoebe, had flown over from London for it but his brother, Peter Jr., was hosting some investors' conference in Palo Alto he couldn't get out of. There was a large contingent of extended family and a smattering of Club, Stratton Mountain and Jupiter Island friends who'd been in the mix since Johnny started walking. The dinner was "seated," which meant some strategy had gone into who sat where. I was slotted between Gwen's sister Brooke and Johnny's cousin Alicia. Brooke was a "Platinum Circle of Excellence" real estate agent in Greenwich who shared Gwen's classic good looks but little of her easy charm. Alicia was about ten years older than me and worked at an auction house in New York. She powered down the white wine like it was the Gatorade for competitive small talk and leaned in close after the umpteenth toast and said, "You really appreciate your Jewish friends when you sit through WASPs trying to be funny, don't you think?"

I laughed at that the way I'd laughed the whole evening, pretending like I got it. All in all, I was doing pretty well until Pete laid a hand on my shoulder as we finished dessert and said to Alicia, "May I steal him for a minute?"

"Only if you promise to bring him right back!" she said, with way more erotic promise than I thought was going on.

"Walk with me, Jeep?" Pete said.

I followed him out onto the vast brick patio overlooking the golf course and the soft spring night.

"I'm so glad you're both in one piece," he said.

"Even the deer got off easy," I said.

"Yes, it's that time of year they start playing 'double dare you' on the roads out here."

I smiled and nodded. He wasn't looking at me, just out over the landscape. He looked like the older Sean Connery, without the facial hair. Everybody said that.

"You know why they named it Two Trees?" he said.

"I do not, actually."

"Legend had it there were a pair of magnificent old American chestnuts somewhere on the back nine where the tribal elders would meet to decide the important issues. Of course, that Indian tribe is long gone and all the American chestnuts were wiped out by a blight, but that's the origin."

"Huh," I managed.

"Do you know why Porsches all have the ignition slot on the left?"

"I'm oh for two," I said. He chuckled politely.

"The legend is so that at Le Mans, where the drivers have to run to their cars and jump in at the start of the race, the driver could start the engine and shift into first at the same time and so shave a second off the line, which could be the margin of victory on the track."

"Wow. Smart," I said.

"But that's the legend. The *fact* is it saved a couple pennies on how they configured the wiring harness. But everyone prints the legend on that one."

I was a little lost, truth be told. Which was how Pete liked it in his dealings with people.

"But back to Friday night? The officer who responded thought maybe it was Johnny driving. Thought Johnny had mud on his shoes, like he'd stepped out the driver's side into the drainage ditch."

I did my best with the split second I had.

"We both would've had mud. We both went around that side to check what was what."

"The officer, Jim Kripinski's his name, good guy, he thought your shoes were clean. And he's sharp."

"Huh" was all I could come up with.

"In business, in life, you want to have good relationships with the boots on the ground. It's the only way you can find out what's really going on around you."

I'd have to remember to get more boots on the ground. I felt ambushed.

"Is Johnny on drugs?" he said, after a moment.

"No, sir."

He waited me out. I lawyered up my answer.

"Not that I know of, and I know Johnny pretty damn well."

"I believe you," he said.

"Thank you, sir. I appreciate that." Which sounded inane, but that's what came out.

"Gwen and I have always been so glad that you're in our son's life. That somehow he's made a good friend who could also be a ballast and a compass. That means the world to us."

"Thank you, Mr. Chambliss. Johnny's one of a kind."

"We're also grateful for your discretion. There're people we both know, a couple of them right there inside, the circumstances of the other night would have been all over town by now if it were one of them in the car."

"Not me."

"I figured. So many people love to trade in gossip, in innuendo and exaggeration. It's like a pandemic these days."

"I guess so."

"That old saying, a lie can travel halfway around the world while the truth is still getting its pants on? Still goes."

I was getting confused again but I just said, "Sure does."

"And not just a lie. A reputation travels fast too. And if someone's plastered yours with dog shit and broken glass, well, that's all she wrote, no matter who you are, who your family is."

The more agitated he got, the lower his voice got, the slower his cadence, like he was sharing something top secret.

He looked at me as if to check that his wisdom had landed. I just nodded, solemn.

"How's your dad doing?" he said.

"Hanging in there, thanks."

"He's a hero in my book. You give him my best."

I think they'd met once, briefly, on the sidelines at the end of a play-off game. I was surprised Mr. Chambliss even remembered.

"I'll do that. Thank you."

"We should get back inside."

I followed him back in. Johnny caught my eye as I started for the bar. I signaled some mild alarm.

Out by the grass tennis courts afterward, I gave him the play-by-play.

"I'm so sorry," Johnny said. "And fuck him."

"Hey listen, my old man would've done some version of the same thing, make sure he had the real story."

"No, he definitely would not have," Johnny said. "Because my father already had the real story. I came clean with him when we went to the shop for estimates the next morning."

"Why?" I said.

"Looking out for you's why. You did me a solid. Who would I be if I paid you back by letting my old man think it was you cracked up the car?"

"You could've. No harm no foul, that play."

"But like I said, what would it make me? A world-class douchebag is what. Plus, then you'd get the shitload of his disapproval and those long speeches on how 'personal accountability' was a 'bedrock principle' of 'the people who mattered.' I'm his son, I *have* to. But I've got twenty years of it under my belt. I'm a pro. You'd be a rookie, and I'd be one lame-ass friend I put you through that as your reward for getting me out of a jam."

My head was spinning a little. One thing stood front and center, though.

"If he already knew, why the whole song and dance about his friend the cop and the mud on the shoes?"

"Exactly. Welcome to my world," he said.

"But why try to smoke someone out, you already know their whole story?"

"Sport," Johnny said. "And a test."

"A test of what?"

"Of can you be trusted to lie *for* a Chambliss, but never lie *to* a Chambliss."

Chapter Six

Jeep wrestled with it the whole drive back to the North Shore. Whether he had a duty to tell them about the ask, or even a choice. Whether it might lighten their load or be another cinder block in their baggage. And whether they should even have a vote; maybe it was their job to just say "of course" and make the arrangements. He was leaning toward keeping it to himself as he drove up West Shore Road along Oyster Bay but the light changed up ahead and he stopped at the intersection and when the light turned green he took the left onto the road that led to the top of the hill.

Jeep parked by the tennis pavilion and got out. The Chambliss home had beautiful views of the sunset to the west, and the view of the house itself was just as stunning; the shadows of the old-growth copper beech and elm trees spilled over the lawns and, in succession, the upper-story windows glowed like lighthouse beacons as the reflection of the sun moved from room to room.

There were two cars parked in the turnaround near the front entrance; they had company. It occurred to Jeep that it might be good manners to wait until their guests had left before intruding and was about to get back into his car when the front door opened, and Pete and

Gwen came out behind the two departing couples. Jeep stepped back into the shadows and watched the round-robin of long hugs and two-hand-squeezes and dabbed-at tears.

The dining room table was covered with a spread of catering trays from the kitchen at the Club; a whole cold salmon and salads and a platter of fanned-out sliced meats and a heated tray of their "famous" truffled mac 'n' cheese and none of them more than slightly dented by the visitors of the day. Gwen wouldn't take no for an answer and was making Jeep a plate as Pete handed him a bourbon on the rocks the size of a medium iced tea.

"Any news?" Gwen said.

"Nothing that points away from 'accident' so far," Jeep said.

"Jeep and his team are backup on this, do I have that right, Jeep?" Pete said.

"Yessir. Nassau PD is running it."

"I still want to hear what Gerald has to say," Gwen said. "Let's sit in the living room."

Gwen and Pete sat on the couch and Jeep in a club chair across from them as he ate some, drank little, and gave the bulletins of the who what where and when. He off-loaded the bourbon and his plate.

Jeep said, "I didn't just come here to update you. And I don't know if someone already came to you with this. But Johnny had a song he wanted played at his funeral."

Pete frowned, Gwen leaned forward. Jeep looked at her with a sad smile.

"Warren Zevon. 'My Ride's Here,'" Jeep said.

She touched her heart and blinked away the tears that sprang up.

"Oh, my," she said.

"Rock and roll at a funeral?" Pete said.

"No sir, it's a ballad. About preparing for death. It's more like a hymn. Even mentions Jesus."

"I gave him the CD to go with the car at graduation," Gwen said.

"I know. He loved it. And though of course it seemed kind of weird to be making your funeral playlist at twenty-three, chalk that up to being Johnny."

Gwen raised her wineglass. "To being Johnny," she said.

Jeep reached for his bourbon and returned her toast and took a small sip.

"I wish we could, I really do," Pete said. "But St. Luke's only allows sacred music at services. I'm pretty sure that's set in stone."

Pete's grandfather's name was also set in stone at St. Luke's, along with the names of the other wealthy New York bankers who'd paid for the church to be built back in the nineteen-teens. It was intended as a kind gesture by the small herd of moneyed men who had bought out the local Quaker farmers and Scots-Irish workmen and turned their small towns and bucolic farms into vast shrines to themselves.

Gwen turned to him. "Surely exceptions can be made."

"Gwen . . ." he said.

"Peter," she said. "It's our son."

"I'm aware. I'm also aware that the Church has its traditions and that Rector Sturdevant is tough that way. If Warren Zevon himself offered to play I don't think they'd accommodate," Pete said.

"He can't. He's dead, too," Gwen said.

She stood up.

"Please excuse me. It's been a long day."

She left the room. Pete and Jeep sat frozen for a moment.

"I'll walk you to your car," Pete said.

Outside, as they crossed the circle to the tennis pavilion, Pete finally spoke again.

"My friend the Attorney General wrote me the most moving note. He said, 'My deepest prayer for you and Gwen and your family is that sooner than you could imagine your sense of grief and loss is pushed to the wings as your very best memories of Johnny take center stage.'"

He slowed to a stop twenty feet from Jeep's car. Jeep turned to him. He had his hands in his pockets and his shoulders hunched.

"Gwen needs that. I need that. And we can use your help."

"Anything I can do," Jeep said.

"My boy is gone, nothing's going to bring him back. The circumstances of his accident may well have some . . . unfortunate elements. I don't know, but I know my son. May have some . . . ingredients that in the wrong hands, the tabloid press, the ambulance-chasing lawyers, the sour-grapes crowd, they could plaster my son's, your *friend's*, reputation with dog shit and broken glass for good. And I don't want that. That would break my heart even more, if that's even possible. So keep a sharp eye out, Jeep. Help this be over. Help us all have those best memories of him come to us quickly."

Jeep didn't know exactly what was being asked of him, only that certain facts of the case might be best left to the tides on the beach in the dark, in Pete Chambliss's estimation.

"Whatever I can," Jeep said.

"Thank you, safe home," Pete said, and turned and walked back to the house.

For the second night in a row Niven's mother's G-Wagen was parked out in front of Jeep's house. He called out for Niven as he walked around the house to the back but there was no reply. There was a quarter moon hanging out, giving enough light to see the pile of her clothes on one of the Adirondack chairs. He called her name again, looking out over the water. He could just make out her form, swimming parallel to the beach about fifty yards out. He cupped his hands around his mouth and called out louder.

"Niven?"

She stopped and treaded water.

"I'll need a towel," she called back.

"Okay," he said.

He went and got a towel from the teak box on the deck and walked down to the water's edge. She swam to about twenty yards offshore and popped up vertical again, standing with the water up to her neck.

"Come on in," she said.

"I'm good."

"Oh, come on. The water's still, like, seventy-something degrees. It's heaven."

"Still good."

"It should be against the law to waste an Indian summer night when you live smack-dab by the sea," she said.

"It *is* against the law to trespass on private property and go naked on the public beaches," he said.

"Are you always this much fun or do I bring it out in you?"

She swam to shore and walked out of the water. Jeep held out the towel and she wrapped it around her and bent over and shook her hair out like a retriever and whipped it back as she stood up.

"I didn't play with Barbies as a little girl and I certainly don't want to look like one as a grown woman," she said.

Jeep feigned some confusion.

"What are you talking about?" he said.

"Pubes," she said. "Don't say you didn't look."

He laughed and shrugged. He also blushed, but it was too dark to see that.

"You hardly ever see any bush in the wild anymore," he said.

"Well, there's a small but growing number of us."

She walked up the steps to his deck and laid the towel on the back of the chair and put her underwear on. Jeep stayed on the sand with his back to her.

"Such a gentleman," she said.

"Just tell me when you're dressed, okay?"

She stepped into her shorts and pulled on her polo shirt.

"All clear, Chief."

Jeep walked back up the steps.

"You want a drink?" he said.

"Whatever beer you've got."

He fetched two from the outdoor stainless mini fridge and handed her one and they sat side by side in the chairs and looked at the water and the moon.

"You've got it good, you know," she said after a moment.

"For a cop?"

"For anybody. You live on the water, I bet you've got your pick of the ladies, and you don't even have to go in the house to grab a beer," she said. "Enjoy every sandwich, Jeep."

Which rang a bell. He looked at her.

"You know who said that?" he said.

"Yeah, Warren Zevon. To David Letterman. About living every moment, like, fully."

Jeep said, "Johnny had a Zevon song he wanted played at his funeral. Did you know that?"

"No."

"First came up the night we cracked up the Porsche. A few times after that, over the years."

Niven guessed, "'Johnny Strikes Up the Band'?"

Jeep said, "No. 'My Ride's Here.'"

"That one's so sad."

She looked at him closely.

"Are you going to tell Pete and Gwen? The funeral's Wednesday."

Jeep said, "I already did."

"And?"

"And according to Pete it's a non-starter."

She shook her head.

"Jesus. What about Gwen?"

Jeep said, "Push come to shove she votes with Pete, the sense I got."

Niven said, "The secret of that happy marriage."

"I get the strong feeling Pete wants this over more than he wants to know what happened."

"How do you mean?" she said.

"He assumes that even if it was just an accident, it would have some details might cause him or them some embarrassment," Jeep said.

"I'd take that bet. Johnny always left some trash in his wake."

"I think Pete was serious. Like, don't go digging up the garden."

"Pete's always serious. Even about golf and cocktails and all the stuff other people do for fun, he can make like it's important work. And reputation is as serious as it gets for him."

"I guess," Jeep said.

"Johnny said his father actually hated dogs but kept them around as alibis in case anyone farted."

They drank some beer. Niven shifted in the chair.

"If you signed an NDA, can you keep things in it from the police?"

Jeep looked at her, trying for a read.

"Asking for a friend?"

Niven said, "Thank you for that. But no, I trust you."

"As far as I know, which isn't that far? Not if it's about a criminal act, or evidence that would pertain to a criminal investigation."

Niven said, "It's not a crime. It's just a secret."

Jeep said, "Who made you sign the NDA?"

She shook her head.

"The less you know . . ."

"I can guess. Good ole Pete. Instead of a pre-nup, or along with a pre-nup?"

Niven said, "You think I should talk to a lawyer?"

"Yes, I do."

Chapter Seven

The county Medical Examiner's office was a dun-colored brick pile on the edge of the University Medical Center in East Meadow. A little before 9:00 A.M. Jeep parked a few slots over from the ME's assigned space. He knew she got to work at exactly 9:00 A.M. because while she didn't mind working late she never came in early because her "clientele," which was what she called the dead bodies, "didn't much care about early birds and worms." Jeep knew this because he and ME Doreen DiMucci had a thing going for about three months the year before. He'd convinced himself that he'd broken it off because he just couldn't shake that the epic sex he was enjoying was with a woman who handled dead people's organs all day. But if he was being honest with himself, which he tried to avoid in this one area, it was because Doreen was a gorgeous, available, funny, intelligent woman who took great joy in pleasing the man in her life and Jeep was somehow hardwired to need them challenging, withholding and mercurial.

She pulled her cherry red Mustang 5.0 into her slot at 8:59 and got out and Jeep timed his own exit perfectly.

"Hey, Doreen."

She turned quickly, on defense. Saw who went with the voice and relaxed.

"Jeep. Whatup?"

"I have a couple questions for you."

Doreen looked him over with some attitude.

"Yes, I am seeing somebody, and no, he's not a cop."

Jeep smiled. "Not about that, though good to know. Lucky guy."

She took it at face value and smiled.

"You're in civvies and driving your own car."

"I'm not here on official duty," Jeep said. "It's about the vic you got Sunday morning."

Doreen said, "Off the Bayville beach?"

"Yes. He was an old friend of mine."

"I'm sorry."

Jeep said, "Thanks. County has the case so I'm just an interested party with some questions."

Doreen said, "And you don't like County's answers?"

Jeep weighed his reply.

"I just get the impression this thing's being goosed along."

"You and me both," she said.

Which is both what he wanted to hear and didn't want to hear, about fifty-fifty.

"Yes, I like it for a boating accident. But your friend had scratches on his shoulders and back from human fingernails. Which don't normally go with boating accidents."

Jeep said, "Like what, from sex?"

"Possibly. But you've had plenty of insane sex in your day, some of it with me. How many times you walk away with your back scratched up?"

Jeep tried to think of the times but it took longer than the time allotted.

Doreen said, "That's about how often I've seen it on the table. The cat trying to wake the croaked old man up, sure. But from, like, Sharon Stone—movie sex, not so much. It wasn't the cause of death but it is a loose thread and I hate those, professionally speaking."

Jeep said, "Can you tell when he got them?"

Doreen said, "Under the microscope there was evidence of neutrophils, which are the white blood cells that act like a body's first responders to a wound, and which arrive in about an hour. But there was no evidence of monocytes, the white cells that take over after about twenty-four hours. So we can figure he got the scratches the day of and possibly the night of."

Jeep thought hard before he asked the next question.

"But you signed off on the cause?"

Doreen sized Jeep up for a moment.

"Yes, I signed off. Cause of death, *undetermined*. And I'm getting pressure to change my vote to 'accidental.' Now, I like my job and I'm good at it so I'm not gonna say from who, not that I don't trust you. But I will tell you what I told them. I said, Bring me a logical explanation for the scratches on his back and shoulders and I'll sign off on 'accidental.' Until then it stands as undetermined pending toxicology results. And no, I don't think he OD'd, either."

Fourteen Years Earlier

The Friday afternoon of Labor Day weekend that year my mom was delayed with my dad at the hospital and Johnny was good to pick me up at the Oyster Bay train station. As was his style, Johnny managed a four- or five-day weekend when everybody else just got the three. I'd cut out early from a job I hated and caught a standing-room-only LIRR train from the rank sauna of Penn Station, and when I hit the platform I took a deep breath like an asthmatic off a hit from the inhaler.

Johnny honked and wheeled over and we caught up on the way out to Bayville. Well, he caught *me* up, with his and Niven's full schedules of tennis and golf and parties at the Club and Sunday's US Open day session at Arthur Ashe Stadium in Queens. I was included in most, I passed on them all. My father had one foot in the grave and the other on a banana peel, as my mom used to say about ailing older friends and acquaintances.

My father was an NYPD homicide detective working Manhattan North when the planes had hit the towers nine years earlier. He and his partner bolted from their squad just after 9:30 that morning but they were still twenty blocks north when the first tower fell and they were turned back. As soon as permitted, my father worked the rubble, looking first for survivors and then for remains, until he collapsed of exhaustion one night after three straight weeks of it and was banned for his own good. Which turned out to be way too little, too late; within a couple years he was diagnosed with the full roster of pulmonary, kidney, lymph and liver diseases, obstructions and tumors that resulted from duty working Ground Zero as time went by. The doctors had played a valiant game of Whac-A-Mole but it was a losing game from early on.

His name was Gerald "Gerry" Patrick Mullane and he was fifty-one years old. He was my compass and my foundation, and my compass was broken and my foundation was crumbling to dust.

When we pulled up, there was a North Shore-LIJ ambulette still in the driveway; one attendant was folding up a wheelchair and the other was talking to my mom, who waved to us but not like waving for us to join.

She said, "Dad's out back."

Johnny looked to me for his cue.

I said, "Come say a quick hello."

We went around back. He was sitting in one of the Adirondack chairs in a short-sleeved shirt that showed bruising and bandages on his wrists and inside his elbows from the shots and the blood draws and a little plastic bracelet with his name and numbers. He looked like a scarecrow of himself.

"Mr. Mullane, how they hangin'?" Johnny called out.

He reached for his walker and I got there fast.

I said, "No, Pop, don't get up," and bent down and hugged him and then gave Johnny his turn.

He said, "Hey, boys!" in a voice that was half its usual volume but with a smile that could still blind the sun. He looked Johnny over like thinking how to bust his balls.

"What, you get a job modeling for Ralph Lauren?"

Johnny was dressed in tennis whites. It wasn't Dad's sharpest but it would do and Johnny fielded right away.

"Nah, they said I was *too* handsome."

Dad wheezed a laugh, warming up.

"On the Job, you make a questionable collar and they bust you for it, you know what you say? 'Boss, I swear, he's guilty of *something!*'" He pointed at Johnny and chirped at me. "That's this one, all day long!"

We all laughed some and Johnny patted my dad on the shoulder.

"I'll leave you two to figure it all out."

My dad said, "Thanks for stopping by. You be good, and if you can't be good—"

"Be careful," Johnny joined in.

He signaled a *talk later* to me and headed off and I jerked the other Adirondack chair a little closer to my dad and sat.

"How you doing?" I said.

"How's it look?" he said.

He gave me his look that said, *no bullshit please.*

"What did the doctors say?" I said.

"To put my affairs in order."

"They actually say that?"

He shook his head as if in wonder.

"They do. Must teach it in medical school."

My mother came out the sliding door from the kitchen.

"Can I get either of you anything?"

I said, "I'm good, Mom, thanks."

"Gerry?" she said.

"Three fingers of Bushmills?"

"You wish," she said.

"There is one actual thing," he said. "The doctors told me to put my affairs in order. So if you could get Elizabeth Hurley on the phone, I need to let her down gently."

Okay, I thought, he's still got game. You could've seen my mother's eyes roll from the next town over.

She said, "You're the worst of the worst," and went back inside.

After she'd slid the glass door shut my father touched my arm.

He said, "Lean in and don't interrupt."

I did as told.

He spoke quietly, purposefully.

He said, "By a week from now I'm going to be so full of drugs I won't even know what day it is. By a month from now I may be gone. That loan I took to help pay for your college—"

He cut me off before I could get a syllable out, fierce.

"I said don't interrupt."

I shut my mouth again.

"There was no loan. Johnny Chambliss paid for it himself. The only thing he asked for in return was that I'd never tell you."

I sat frozen for a moment. He watched me closely.

He said, "Of course I refused the money. Of course I said we didn't need that kind of help, that I didn't make Chambliss money but made a good and honest living."

I said, "May I *please* speak?"

"Go ahead."

"Why'd you take it?"

"Because of *why* he wanted to give it. Because he said to me, and I'm pretty much quoting him, 'I don't really contribute anything of value to anybody. I try to be a good friend and person but end of the day I'll always be a shallow spoiled fuck compared to most people, especially people like you.' Meaning us, you and me and your mother. And I may not be the best judge of character but I've had my share of good calls. And this was a young man crying out for help and the only help he was asking for was to help pay for your college education and to give my wallet a break. Not even lunch money to him, he said. But that it would make a huge difference in his life. And Jeep, I believed him. I believe it was the right thing to do, and you were me that day, I think you would've done the same thing."

After a while I said, "If I can't thank him then why are you telling me this?"

"Because maybe one day it'll be useful to you. That the lowliest beggar on the streets of Calcutta could be a snobby asshole and the silver spoon rich kid in the mansion on the hill could have a good and humble heart. So maybe you think to always look twice."

We sat there for a long time, watching the birds over the water, saying nothing.

My father was off by a couple months; he hung on until just before Thanksgiving. In December of that year I took the test and was accepted into the next class for the NYPD Police Academy. I had it in my mind to try and pick up where he'd left off. I knew I could never be him but thought maybe I could be *like* him. And I came close to telling Johnny that I knew a couple of times, once out of gratitude and once out of humiliation. But I kept his secret, for my old man's sake.

Chapter Eight

Detective Sam Wong liked to remind anyone who would listen that he was so good at hacking all kinds of computer systems he would be a very rich man if he'd chosen to work the other side of the street.

"I could be sending you this from poolside in Saint-Tropez," Wong said.

He pushed a thumb drive into the side of his laptop.

Jeep said, "Then why are you walking me through it live from Mineola?"

"I was raised to be an honest man. It's a blessing and a curse."

This for like, the hundredth time. A grid of cell phone camera snaps appeared on the screen.

"They turned off location services so no time or date stamps. Just a lot of land yachts and sports cars out in the wild."

Jeep said, "I've been cruising this island forever. Roll 'em."

Wong clicked through a succession of photos and Jeep gave a play-by-play. They were all of high-end automobiles in public spaces, mostly day, some night.

Jeep said, "Americana Mall, valet at Rothmann's Steakhouse,

Americana, Wheatley Plaza, valet at Hendrick's in Roslyn, Wheatley, Americana, Walt Whitman Mall. This Mercedes, where's that?"

Jeep leaned in closer. The still life was of a two-tone AMG SL 63.

"Jesus H. Christ. It's parked by Oncology at NYU-Langone, you can see the entrance there."

He touched the screen at signage in the background.

Jeep said, "How low can you go? Guy's getting chemo or some shit and you're casing his car?"

Wong flipped through a few more.

"Anyway, you get the idea," Wong said.

He dropped down the menu and clicked and the screen swiped to a readout of the call logs.

"To and from other burners. The account for the phone traces back to a Mail Boxes Etc. in Santiago, Chile."

He hit the menu again and Spanish filled the screen.

"Text messages. I can make a straight translation but it's just generic computer Spanish. It's probably in a dialect, you'll need a pro if this is going to be evidence in court."

He scanned the menu again and clicked. The words transformed to English in a blink.

Wong said, "It mostly just matches up with the photographs, price quotes for the cars and ETAs for delivery. But there's something else threaded through, kind of a 'Where's Waldo' about a guy named Angel."

Wong fingered some lines mid-screen.

Wong said, "Seems this Angel boosted a Porsche and never made it to Newark. So he's either in custody or in the wind and these hornets are all stirred up."

Jeep said, "Huh."

Wong pulled the thumb drive and handed it to Jeep.

"I'll make the copy for Nassau PD, save you the trouble," Wong said.

Jeep knew that would be protocol. Jeep needed a bigger favor than the extraction.

Jeep said, "Thanks, but let's put a pin in it for now."

Wong spun around in his chair and faced Jeep.

Wong said, "Not sure I can do that, Jeep."

Jeep said, "Okay, Sam. I'm just asking, I'm not telling."

When Jeep and Wong were both NYPD, Wong was with the Technical Assistance Response Unit working his magic out of One Police Plaza. When Jeep worked Narcotics he did a lot of business with Wong, cell phones and laptops being tools of that trade too, and scored a few times with some terrifically entertaining surveillance options that Wong invented. When Jeep noticed Wong taking it in stride when the Chinaman jokes came around from the guys at the bar or the retirement racket, he asked Wong about it and Wong just shrugged and said, "Goes with the territory." Wong stood about five-seven, weighed maybe one-thirty-five after Thanksgiving dinner, and bird-watched for a hobby in a cop land full of hairbags and ballbusters; his territory was rough enough already without the racist beanballs.

So Jeep called in some of his father's chips, who leaned on some guys who leaned on some other guys and Wong never heard that slanty bullshit again. If Wong knew the who and the how of the ceasefire, he never mentioned it to Jeep.

Wong said, "Okay. You're the chief, Chief. But mind my asking why?"

Jeep said, "It were the other way around, think they'd make one for me?"

Wong eyeballed Jeep with a smile and shook his head.

"No way."

"If this can of worms opens from the inside, I'd like to be the first one in."

Chapter Nine

Jeep had changed into his dress uniform for a press conference that was
held outside his trailer at headquarters. "Press conference" was maybe
a little grand for what it was. The press contingent consisted of a perky
blonde from News 12 Long Island ("As local as local news gets!"), a
cub reporter for the *North Shore Leader* ("The Leading News Source for
Long Island's Gold Coast, over 77 Years!"), and a stringer for *Newsday*
who looked like he'd slept in his car. News 12 had brought the one
camera crew, as they broadcast twenty-four hours a day and needed all
the footage they could get. Jeep gave anodyne boilerplate answers to
their questions about the wave of auto thefts and said nothing about the
investigation into Johnny's death because none of them asked a single
question about it.

The Elgin-Ford Funeral Home had been catering to prominent corpses
and their families in the area since 1915. Up until that time, the wakes
for the departed were held at home, with all the attendant work and
stress that made for the grieving survivors. Elgin and Ford had bought
the house next door to their modest facility and fashioned the entire

first floor into an accommodating large parlor complete with wet bar and a small service kitchen. It was an immediate hit with the local gentry and the business grew quickly, but Elgin and Ford liked to think they thought "big." So when news came of a death in one of the most prominent families with a country home in the area, the elegant Mr. Elgin solicited them to consider having the services out there instead of the usual Manhattan routing of Frank E. Campbell Funeral Home to the Cathedral of Saint John the Divine. He stressed how happy the departed would be to know that friends and family gathered to mourn and remember him not in dirty New York City but in the pastoral splendor of the area where he built Poise 'n Ivy or Sans Souci or whatever name headed the stationery stocked in the guest rooms at the estate. By 1920 they had a lock on the dearly departed of the monied class out there and the Elgin-Ford Funeral Home was referred by those in the know the way certain florists and portrait photographers and holiday destinations were; like a listing in a little blue book that could have been titled *How to* Really *Be Rich.*

Johnny would have been making morbid jokes but Johnny was in the closed casket on a catafalque at the far end of the parlor. Jeep took another step forward as the line to the casket moved up a place. He nodded to a few friends and acquaintances sitting in the folding chairs, either locked in whispered conversation or checking out who else had made the scene. Beyond the casket a second line had formed to clasp and hug and murmur to Pete and Gwen and Peter Jr. and Phoebe. On deck were County Executive Trace Barnett and District Assemblywoman Claire Ireland. Pete Chambliss's idea of "boots on the ground" included the higher elevations.

Niven appeared beside him.

"Hey."

"Hey."

"I'm cutting the line. It's out the door by, like, twenty feet."

"You're the widow. You can jump all the way to the front if you want," Jeep said.

Niven returned some discreet waves to people she knew, which took a while.

Niven said, "When one of those real bastard old-time movie moguls died, Louis B. Mayer I think, hundreds and hundreds showed up and one of his employees says to another, 'Some turnout, huh?' and the other guy goes, 'Like he'd say, give the people what they want and they'll come out to see it.'"

Jeep said, "That how you're feeling today?"

Niven said, "When I feel like I'm gonna lose it again I remind myself the reasons I have to hate him."

"That working for you?"

"Off and on. Nice uniform."

Jeep had planned to change into a suit after the press conference but it occurred to him that this tribe buried its sudden, younger deaths with a minimum of fanfare, occurring as they largely did under muddy circumstances like single-car accidents and prescription drug dosage "miscalculations" or even late-night "tragic boating mishaps." For a *Pete* Chambliss funeral it would be standing room only with senators and congressmen in somber suits sporting American flag lapel pins, CEOs and a couple Ivy League university presidents, the beloved old bartender at the Club and the current heads of local land and architectural preservation outfits, all in their finest, all honoring a legacy, all comforting each other with *he had a great run.*

But his son Johnny was thirty-eight and had yet to stock much of a legacy, and even his own father had made it clear that the less pomp the better, given the circumstances. Barnett's and Ireland's presence was a wild card, Jeep thought; likely showing up out of fealty to a deep-pocketed donor but with an outside chance they were helping the family bring about a speedy "closure."

"It's my dress uniform."

"You throwing a parade for him?"

He shot her a look. It landed.

"Sorry. You look very nice."

Jeep said, "Just thought it might bring more gravity and respect than my Men's Wearhouse blue suit."

"My bitter ex-wife uniform is at the cleaner's or I would've," she said.

Jeep just nodded. She slid him a look.

"Good for you," she said, without any spin.

"You look nice too."

Niven wore a dark green blazer and matching skirt and whatever scent Jo Malone of London sold as appropriate for solemn occasions. She smelled great, if in fact it was her and not one of the thousands of flowers in the room.

Jeep said, "I haven't cried yet. Not once. How come?"

She looked at him like he was kidding and then, seeing he wasn't, with genuine empathy.

She said, "Because if one of you ever cried the other one would bust his balls and maybe that's what holds you back, but when you have the moment you admit he's really gone then you will."

She took his hand in hers. Jeep took the opportunity to look down and check out her fingernails. They were manicured and polished and did not appear to have human tissue packed under them. He shook it off and gently let her hand go as they stepped before the casket.

Niven said, "You go first. Don't argue."

Jeep kneeled down on the pad. He put his hand on the casket. He remembered that the last time he'd seen his friend he was The Man Without a Face. He shook it off. He took in the elaborate flower arrangements crowding the casket and packed like a bamboo grove against the wall. He bent over, inches from the wood, and whispered.

"Place looks like you won the Kentucky fucking Derby."

He waited for a laugh that did not come and then for tears that did not come so he gave up and joined the receiving line for the family.

Once outside, Jeep buttoned on his radio and checked in with base as he thumbed the messages icon on his cell phone screen. All Quiet on the Gold Coast Front.

He noticed Coach's mid-aughts Dodge Ram pickup rash a tire as he parked at the curb. The logo and digits of his eponymous contracting company stenciled on the door were gouged and scratched and badly in need of a refresh. Coach got out, a little unsteady, and chirped the lock with the key fob, then started for the entrance with a slight weave to his gait.

Jeep called out, "Hey, Coach!"

Coach waved back but stayed straight for the entrance. Jeep changed course and intercepted him, his gut kicking in.

Jeep said, "How you doing, good?" It was the customary Lawn Guyland greeting, the gold standard of neighborly good manners for the regular folks.

"Good, you?" Coach said.

"Good."

"Good," Coach said, right on cue.

"How's the family, good?" Jeep continued.

"Got divorced a couple years ago," Coach said.

Which set off alarms in Jeep. The "good?" tag was there as a preemptive. Common courtesy demanded a rigorous adherence to the script. It did not allow for deviations into actual health or family problems. Everyone was busy enough with their own shit.

Jeep pivoted, gesturing to the funeral home.

Jeep said, "Helluva thing, huh?"

Coach said, "Helluva thing, all right. One helluva thing."

Clearly five o'clock had come way early for Coach that day; Jeep could smell the whiskey on the gust of his breath. He was wearing a shirt and tie under his Jeep-and-Johnny era Long Island Cannons wind-breaker.

Jeep touched the "Coach" embroidered on the chest.

"Respect," Jeep said, taking his temperature.

"I know you two were still friends, but fuck him," Coach said.

By his midtwenties Johnny had put some of his trust-fund money into identifying, restoring and flipping local brick piles and tumble-downs. With some early guidance from his mother he became an ace stock-picker in what properties had the hidden value and marketable history that was catnip to the new money that wanted to arrive as old, or at least not as money printed that morning. They were plum jobs for the local general contractors; between the research hours and the custom-milled restoration requirements you could pad the ledger like a cop banking overtime as his pension cutoff drew near. Coach was al-ways knocking on Johnny's door and Coach was awarded exactly none of the contracts.

Coach said, "Just last year, the old Chapin house on Horseneck Road? I underbid everybody. I know, 'cause I asked around. I went so low that when I broke it down to myself I saw I'd be clearing twenty-five an hour, I was lucky. And he said, Lower. And I went lower, 'cause that kind of job turns into others of that kind of job. And I, you know, confided; I'm behind on the alimony and child care, give a guy a break, old time's sake. End of the day he went with the Cummings brothers at a higher bid and I went back to him and I went 'Why?' and he looked me right in the eye and he said, 'I heard you were *careless*,' and then he laughed at his own joke."

Jeep stayed still and looked sympathetic.

"I mean Jesus, we had nicknames for everybody!" Coach said.

Jeep said, "What was mine?"

Coach shook his head. "You already had one."

Jeep held his gaze, now in full-on community-policing de-escalation mode.

"Bygones be bygones," Jeep said.

"Easy for you to say."

"What are you doing here, Coach?"

"Just closing the book."

Coach took a step back and turned away and headed for the front door of the funeral home. The first viewing session hours were drawing to a close; if there was still a line, it ended inside.

Jeep hurried around back and found the service entrance and went inside and took up a post by the side door to the reception room in full view of the casket but partly obscured by the stands of flowers.

The Chambliss family was still fully engaged with contemporaries offering condolences; Niven was sitting with a small bunch in the folding chairs, her arm around Lisbet Woodard, all in a somber huddle.

Coach knelt in front of the casket, arms folded across his chest like he did when he'd ream you for a misplay on the field. His lips moved but no sound came out.

Coach steadied himself with his hands on the casket and pushed off and got to his feet.

He racked a gob of phlegm and spat it on the casket just as Jeep reached his side, and everyone turned and looked at them. Jeep gripped Coach's arm and swiped the stain with a handkerchief and got right in Coach's ear, all in one fell swoop.

"You so much as hiccup I'll bust you for assaulting the chief of police," Jeep said, low and fast.

Jeep hustled him out the side entrance and into the parking lot.

"*Now* bygones be bygones," Coach said.

Jeep kept right on marching him.

"I'm going to drop you home; you're clearly over the limit and not just alcohol."

"Hey, a little respect?" Coach said, like a brat whining.

"You get respect when you show respect. I don't want to hear another word out of you," Jeep said.

Jeep checked Coach's fingernails as he ducked him into the back of the Explorer. They were chipped and dirty and told Jeep nothing except that maybe he really was looking to solve a simple act of fate.

They drove in silence except for the questions in Jeep's head. "Spitting on a casket, who does that?" was easy; it was the fifty-five-year-old bitter drunk sitting in back did that. The harder questions were "What *really* made him to do that?" and "What *else* don't I see?"

Jeep pulled up in front of Coach's rented house in Glen Cove. It was a tired split-level that might as well have been called Rancho Solo. Jeep hauled Coach out of the back seat with a yank.

"They got cameras all over the cemeteries these days on account of the swastikas getting sprayed on headstones. You thinking about pissing on his grave, think twice, 'cause I'll find out."

"Ain't gonna."

"Better not."

Coach started up the cracked flagstone walk to the door and turned back.

"Hey, Jeep," he said. "You were always a good kid. Head on your shoulders. Why'd you stay mixed-up with that crowd?"

"I'm not *mixed-up*," Jeep said.

"Yeah, you are. Always have been. You think they're your friends but they think you're their novelty item, a bobblehead doll. But you never wanted to see it."

He continued up the walk and disappeared into his sad rental. Jeep got into his car and shook off a distant ring of truth and drove away.

Thirteen Years Earlier

Without me knowing, it had been arranged that the party for my graduation from the Police Academy would be held at Brookside, the other exclusive country club in the area, the one Niven had belonged to since childhood. Two Trees and Brookside were a couple of miles apart and both almost a hundred years old. Brookside had been founded when enough bigwigs and pooh-bahs had been turned down for membership at Two Trees and decided to start a restricted club of their own. Those Two Trees rejects weren't Jewish or Black or of any other obvious Otherness; they just didn't make the cut and the reasons could be guessed at but would never be codified or recorded.

A hundred years later it was impossible to tell the difference between the members of one club or the other; if you took a group portrait of both rosters at their conjoined annual Fourth of July fireworks celebration, your only question would be "Where do they keep the ugly children?"

It was customary for the Johnnys and Nivens of that tribe to become Junior Members of the clubs they grew up in. It was also customary, if a couple were members of one and the other, to "spread the wealth" when it came to dining, sports, private parties and the more important dinner-dances at each establishment. So a coin was flipped or a ledger was balanced and it was Brookside that won the lottery to host my do.

The trouble started with *our* side's interpretations of the dress code for a club like Brookside. Johnny's and Niven's parents and siblings, as well as the friendlies from Locust Valley High and Shelter Rock who were still in our orbits, showed up in the blazers and khakis or print dresses that they knew to be the standard uniform for a late-afternoon cocktail reception at a club. Our side, mostly a collection of aunts and uncles from the boroughs or North Jersey and a couple dozen of my dad's crew from the NYPD and their spouses, split about sixty-forty between correct for Princess Diana's funeral and for a midnight screening of *Caddyshack*.

As they arrived, the men scoped the room and whipped off their ties or gave mortified looks to their wives; the women mostly tried to disappear, and failing that, pasted on brave smiles. They took in the surroundings with a mix of awe and fear.

I went into action like some cruise-ship activities director with his job on the line, making introductions, accepting congratulations. After a couple drinks and some food the crowd settled down some and the toasts went a ways to putting the focus on me.

Johnny and Niven gave a tandem recounting of stories from over the years and how the betting line on me becoming a cop or a criminal had always been dead-even odds. Like the best toasts, it had just enough exaggeration to be genuinely funny and just enough misty sentiment to bring *awwww*s from the assembled.

My mom's toast was short and sweet and shy, just like my mom when she had to stand up and speak in public. And my dad's longest-running partner, Deputy Chief Dan O'Connor's, was a hilarious take on how cops raised their kids, until he got to the part about how proud my old man would be if he were here, at which point he lost his battle with his emotions and the tears came and he choked up so I stepped in and hugged him and handed him off to the missus.

I toasted them all back and warned the first-timers that at clubs like Brookside they had metal detectors on the way *out* so to leave the silver-ware on the premises.

Afterward, I took a lap of the knots and huddles. I stayed as Detective Jimmy Nardozzi, another partner and old pal of my dad's, was holding forth by the fireplace with probably his third yarn and with his fourth Scotch in hand. He was telling a war story from his rookie year on foot patrol; trying to arrest a cross-dresser who had an outstanding warrant for attempted murder.

"Anyways, I tell him I'm placing him under and he turns around and puts his mitts on the glass—we're in front of the Colony Records in Times Square, like a whole city block of plate glass? Anyways, I get the cuffs out and I go to take one hand and *boom!* He kicks back and whacks me one good and we're off to the races! Now, this guy is about six-three, two-thirty and all muscle under that dress, and I'm, well, hey, you're looking at it! Long story short, a crowd gathers and of course it looks like a cop, *me*, is assaulting a lady in the middle of the sidewalk! So they start screaming at me in like five different languages *leave her alone!* and now this motherfucker's got me in a headlock and I'm yelling 'That's no lady!' and I finally get out from under and figure I'll prove it and I go to pull off the wig and he tosses me into the plate glass and goes 'YOU NEVER TOUCH A LADY'S HAIR!'"

That last in a high-pitched screech. Johnny and Niven, the mutual friendlies they invited, the other cops and their wives, all laughed their asses off.

Pete Chambliss, Niven's parents, Hugh and Adrienne, and their friendlies smiled politely, which was an improvement on the winces and grimaces they shot each other during the telling.

I know, because I was clocking it.

I didn't hold a lot of things to be absolute truths, that seemed like a road that usually dead-ends in disappointment and worse. But I thought one thing was true. You have a room with a senator, a rock star, a brain surgeon, an astronaut, a famous actor, and a big-city cop? Within ten minutes the first five are all begging the cop for another story. Cops don't tell anecdotes dropping bold-faced names or epic feats; they forge grinding desperation and heartbreak into twisty human comedies. They digest the worst in humanity every day and they tell those stories to bleed the pipes. And if you can't recognize and value that, you're seriously lacking in humanity yourself.

Which is what I wanted to say to Pete and his friends but I was the guest of honor plus my mom was there so I just hoped Jimmy Nardozzi hadn't noticed and I went outside for some air.

Johnny came up behind me.

"You thinking this was a dumb idea?"

"What, the party?" I said.

"Having it *here*."

"It's beautiful here," I said.

"Cut the shit. Your people never looked that grim at an open bar, ever."

"They were maybe a little overwhelmed when they first got here. You gotta understand, they've never been at a club like this. It's like a foreign country."

"That ain't it," he said.

"What ain't what?"

"That Nardozzi knows he says 'motherfucker' a bunch of times in that kind of company he's poking a bear."

"He wasn't poking a bear. That's just him getting caught up in the telling."

"I thought Niven's mom was going to warn *language* to him. Like she would to Niven saying *douchebag* at a family dinner."

We laughed at that. Johnny quit first.

"Porter Sandwick told your mom that the reason there's no pictures of Michelle Obama pregnant is 'cause she's a transexual and their kids are from some African trafficking ring," he said.

"Seriously?"

"That's what my mom's trying to talk her off a ledge about."

My mother was a staunch Republican but an even stauncher decent human being.

"Jesus," I said. I looked over. The two of them were still alone at the edge of the patio.

"It has nothing to do with class or money and everything to do with marking your spot like the dog."

I slid him a sour look. "So *that's* how the world works!" I had zero patience for when Johnny started explaining it all for you. Now, usually, he'd just eat it and make a joke. That day he gave a look like he was about to throw a punch.

"The real toast I wanted to make? Starts 'Hey, Jeep, wise the fuck up.' There's such a thing as *too* nice a guy. You go around that city in that uniform with a gooey marshmallow center looking for the best in people? Next one of these'll be your funeral."

"Fuck you, man," I said. And I fucking meant it.

"Fuck me, fine. But you need to hear it and I don't mean that 'brothers in blue, we got your back' sentimental bullshit at the ceremony. You're a good and decent man and you walk around assuming down deep everyone's got a kernel of that, just waiting for you to bring it out. They don't. Forget that. Get more cynical than the next guy."

"Even if the next guy's you?"

"Yeah."

This was the first time I wanted to call him out for picking up my tuition. Give the lie to this hard-ass bullshit. Kick the legs out from under that pose. But I'd made a promise to my old man, and the promise was based on looking for the good in people, being patient for their best selves to make an appearance.

"Why you doing this?" I said.

"I'm trying to be your friend," he said.

"No, my friend and his girlfriend threw me this little soiree. You're some asshole trying to ruin it."

He laughed a little, at himself.

"I meant what I said. But you do got me on the 'why now.'"

He looked over at our mothers. They were laughing, probably about some shit one of us had pulled.

"You're a New York City cop now. We're not going to see each other much, that's just how that goes. Out here we had a lot of natural intersections. Not so much going forward, unless I take up robbing banks in your precinct and I'd suck at that, so . . ."

He broke off, shrugged and grinned.

"It's thirty miles away, plus you're always in and out with Niven working there," I said.

"It's also a million miles away, in a way," he said.

And I knew he was right; I hadn't thought bigger picture. I'd just been inducted into a whole other tribe.

"So this is what, my going-away party?"

"Nah. We'll always be friends. I just won't be around to pick up after your messes as much, so be careful out there."

He held up a hand, I high-fived it.

"Let's go see what the moms have cooked up for Porter Sandwick," he said.

Chapter Ten

Jeep was standing behind Corporal Jackson at her desk looking over her shoulder at a Google Earth map on her monitor. He'd tasked her with taking a deep dive into the thumb drive from Wong, as she was certified bilingual by the NYPD. Her first post had been in Washington Heights in Upper Manhattan and, being a sharp and eager rookie, she had learned as many dialects of the Spanish language as her brain could hold, which turned out to be a lot. After transcribing the texts to, from and regarding "Angel" she'd rummaged around and found a cache of maps. She talked a mile a minute, as usual.

"This one's of the LIRR service road runs parallel to the tracks to the north and Duck Pond Road to the south."

The map had been annotated with little red arrows, like virtual versions of the little stickers showing where to sign on a lease.

She continued, "The arrows are pretty self-explanatory, they mark houses whose backyards border the service road that, per Zillow, range in value from two-point-one to five-point-two million."

Jeep said, "'Self-explanatory' means you don't have to explain."

"Copy that, Chief."

At Jeep's direction, Corporal Jackson had started using the real estate website Zillow to define neighborhoods' potential value to criminals by entering addresses in the search engine, giving them an up-to-date rich-o-meter. Jeep figured the criminal class might be using the same metric to "Zestimate" the value of the contents of homes and garages they didn't have eyeball access to. You can't steal a house but everything in it is theoretically portable and sure they were shots in the dark but you never know.

She clicked the mouse and another annotated Google Earth map appeared.

Jeep said, "The Water District fire road by Beaver Creek and dam."

Jackson said, "They got our whole precinct sectored out like one of those cuts-of-meat diagrams of a cow."

"Yeah, and we're all strip steaks and T-bones."

"Good one, Chief," she said.

"Effing Google Earth, every restricted two-track in the world and where you can enter and exit's available to any and every crook and lowlife looking to score," Jeep said.

"All respect, Chief, you sound like some old white dude bitching about the music."

Sergeant Bondurant knocked and entered at the same time.

"Quiet night out there so Officer Diaz put the CBAF up over the Land Trust trail backs up to the Knollwood Estates," he said.

CBAF stood for Centre Brookville Air Force and was the acronym Jeep had given to the single surveillance drone they'd been issued. The Knollwood Estates was a four-acre zoned, gated community carved from the swath of some robber baron's torn-down palace from a century ago. One house had sold to a software developer for five-point-two million the previous summer.

Jeep said, "But wait, there's more?"

"Yeah, sorry, drone's got eyes on an SUV in there and Diaz wants to know should he fly the drone down for a better look but risk getting spotted?"

"Motorized vehicles on Land Trust trails is in our books, right?" Jeep said.

Jackson said, "Two and four wheels prohibited, penalty fines and prosecution."

Bondurant said, "So that's a yes, send her in?"

Jeep said, "That's a no. We'll go in ourselves."

Jackson said, "We're going to bust a grand theft auto ring for trespassing?"

Jeep said, "We're going to try and put a dent in them any way we can. And not for nothing, they got Al Capone on back taxes."

Bondurant nodded. Jackson had a follow-up question.

"Who's Al Capone again?"

Most of the public roads north of Route 25A were tricky by day and borderline hazardous by night. They swooped and curved without much topographic rhyme or reason and had no shoulders or sidewalks to offer a margin of error before the boulders and berms and vegetation rose up to strake the passenger-side door or swipe the side-view mirror. They had names like Skunks Misery and Chicken Valley and Roger Canoe Hollow that seemed like drunk-history translations from the original Native American place-names. But for Jeep and his colleagues, the worst part was that this platter of noodles made high-speed pursuit of fleeing bad guys impossible, which crushed one of the reasons they all went on the Job in the first place: to play cops and robbers in real life.

Jeep and Bondurant took the south entrance to the trail off Rabbit Fever Lane and Jackson and Diaz crept in from the north. The trail was groomed, a half moon in the clear night sky gave enough illumination to proceed without headlights announcing them.

The plan was to pincer the car-theft crew in a blockade and so do a little meet and greet and even take a little police action, should the Archangel Michael smile down on them that night.

They rounded a bend and stopped, and Jeep made a chopping motion to Bondurant in the direction of four figures hanging around a silver SUV about fifty yards ahead.

"I see 'em," Bondurant said.

Jeep turned the radio volume down to barely audible and picked up the handset.

"We're point eight miles in. You?"

"Point six," Diaz responded.

Bondurant consulted the map up on his iPad.

"Puts the rustlers dead center between us."

Jeep let it go, given the urgency at hand. He held the radio mouthpiece close.

"They're about seventy yards to your south. On three, light 'em up."

Jeep replaced the handset, waited a beat, flipped the headlights on, hit the roof light–bar toggle and accelerated as Bondurant reached for two Maglites. He could see Diaz and Jackson's lights strobing the trees from up the rise.

He skidded to a stop and his stomach dropped as he recognized Mayor Donahue turning toward them, pinned in the headlights, his mouth open and arms outstretched and palms turned up in the universal sign for *What the fuck?!*

Diaz pulled up hot. Diaz was the department's youngest cop and would pull up hot to a Wendy's drive-through window, just for fun. He and Jackson jumped out and brought their Maglites up to their ears and lit up the "suspects."

Jeep and Bondurant assumed the same positions.

"Police! Stand where you are and put your hands on your heads!" Jeep barked.

Nobody moved, but nobody put their hands on their heads, either.

"NOW!" Jeep said.

Two of the four complied. Donahue wasn't one of them.

He said, "For fuck's sake, Mullane, it's me. Me and Pitch Sterling and—"

"GUN!" Jackson yelled.

All four of the Centre Brookville PD drew theirs, as per training. For Jackson and Diaz it was for the first time ever in the line of duty.

"DROP IT! NOW!" Jackson yelled.

A chubby guy in a polo shirt and seersucker shorts let the shotgun at his side fall to the ground and laced his fingers on his head.

"It's a hundred-thousand-dollar Purdey!" he said.

"Bert, shut up!" Donahue said.

"It's not supposed to lay on the ground!" Bert said.

"Everybody stop talking!" Jeep said, cutting him off.

A silence fell. Blue strobe lights lit eight expressions ranging from fear to astonishment to disgust.

"Is anyone else armed?" Jeep said.

"There's a couple more shotguns in the back of the car," Donahue said.

Jackson and Diaz backed up to the vehicle, weapons still at ready position.

"Armed on their *person*," Jeep said.

Three no's came back.

"You're looking at four of the best shots at the range at Two Trees. We know our way around guns, nothing to worry about," Donahue said.

Jeep realized that he was also looking at the mayor's windbreaker, which had his name stenciled under the village seal on the chest.

"Does that jacket say 'Mayor' in big letters on the back?" Jeep asked.

"Matter of fact, it does," Donahue said.

Jeep didn't know whether to laugh or cry so he just holstered his weapon and his officers followed suit.

"This is a Land Trust trail. There are no motorized vehicles allowed.

There are plenty of signs posted. You are in violation of the law by being out here in that truck," Jeep said as calmly as he could manage.

If Donahue were a cartoon character just then, he was Hector the Bulldog puffing himself up to show Sylvester the Cat just who was boss.

"Seems to me the violation of the law happening here is my police rounding up citizens instead of criminals."

"Is that right," Jeep said.

"Yes. Pitch and Spence and Bert and I are out here as a citizen militia trying to aid in the defense against a crime wave of property theft that's gone from bad to worse. We stand as a dynamic, *dynamic* example of Sir Robert Peel's principles of community policing."

Here we go, Jeep thought.

Sir Robert Peel was an early-nineteenth-century British Home Secretary whose Metropolitan Police Act of 1829 established a full-time, disciplined police force in the Greater London area. His Nine Principles of Policing, the most often quoted of which is *the police are the public and the public are the police*, are as widely and conveniently misinterpreted as the Holy Bible and the United States Constitution.

Jeep made a split-second calculation regarding his next move, pinballing between hauling them in, throttling the mayor, and tossing his shield to the ground and quitting right then and there.

"Sergeant Bondurant, secure that shotgun with the other weapons in the vehicle here and take Corporal Jackson and Corporal Diaz back to Command in ours."

Bondurant moved for the Purdey. Jeep found the eyes of Bert, Spence and Pitch.

"You gentlemen will be issued summonses and fined the maximum one thousand dollars for off-roading on Land Trust property, prompt payment most appreciated. Please get in your vehicle and follow my officers back to the public roads."

They started for the SUV, including Donahue.

"Mayor Donahue, you stay. I'll drop you home."

"Why me?"

Jeep just waited him out. Once again, it didn't take long.

Donahue said, "I just don't think I like the sound of that."

Jeep said, "And I just think it's best we speak privately, as Mayor and Chief of Police, while the events are still fresh in our minds."

Jeep got so still he didn't even breathe or blink, his gaze pinned on Donahue.

Bert, Spence and Pitch made for the SUV, all but sneaking away on tiptoes like Sylvester past a snoring Hector's doghouse. Bondurant, Diaz and Jackson boarded the Explorer. Six doors slammed closed and the convoy rolled off.

Donahue shifted a little, trying for a casual *waiting for the others to putt out* look, mostly failing as Jeep just kept his eyes pinned.

"So what did you want to talk about?" Donahue said.

Jeep shook his head. "Oh, let's see, where to start? Respect for the uniform, the chain of command, heck, the *law* itself? The fact that we are not at the shooting range at your Club and these perps are not clay pigeons? The 'not a good look for *you*' scenario where you fire me or I quit just nine months into the job on account of you seem to think you're a better cop than I am? Or how about that fucking ridiculous windbreaker, like you're riding up front on *Blue Bloods*?"

Donahue defaulted back to his puffed-up, chin-jut pose.

He said, "Fine. Let's talk."

"We just did."

Jeep turned away and headed for the Explorer. Mayor Donahue hustled a quick review of his options and followed.

After dropping Donahue, Jeep swung by the strip mall near the Locust Valley-Glen Cove line where there was a Subway franchise and a Buy Rite liquors conveniently located right next door to each other. He ordered up a foot-long double-meat capicola and provolone piled so high with lettuce, tomatoes, peppers and onions that it also counted as a healthy salad and then next door bought a pint of Maker's Mark that counted as his reward for surviving such a soul-sucking day.

As Jeep pulled into his driveway he lost a bet with himself, having picked *not* on whether or not Niven would be lying in wait again. The G-Wagen was parked in what was fast becoming its usual spot. He shut off the car, peeled back the wrapping on one end of the sandwich, bit off a couple inches, uncapped the bottle, and washed the bite down with a significant swallow of whiskey. Fortified, he got out and went around back.

Chapter Eleven

They sat in the Adirondack chairs sharing the sandwich and taking turns with the whiskey. A side effect of the events of the last couple days had made eating a feast-or-famine proposition for both of them; you forgot to eat until there was actual food within reach and you realized you'd gone twelve hours on a handful of Fritos or something. When Jeep had enough of the hero in his stomach and the whiskey in his brain he cast out a line.

"Niven, what are you doing here?"

She frowned, as if hurt by the question.

"I need a reason?"

"Three nights in a row, unannounced? Yeah," he said.

She tried to keep the hurt look going, gave up.

"Honestly?" she said.

"That'd be nice," he said.

"You ever see *Wedding Crashers*?" she said.

"Of course. A couple times," Jeep said.

"That part toward the end, where Vince Vaughn is so messed up he crashes a *funeral* with Will Ferrell 'cause Will Ferrell convinces him to branch out to funerals 'cause women at funerals are all real vulnerable and easy marks? Well, that always struck me as probably true in real life."

"Okay. I can see that," he said. "So, you're here looking for a roll in the hay?"

"No."

"Then which is it?" he said.

"Which is what?" She flashed him a little annoyance. But Jeep was over and done with other people's personal agendas for the day and so just soldiered on.

"That a woman might be looking for some sexual distraction out of grief might play as a surprise in a comedy movie but not so much in real life. You said *honestly?* and I said yes. So tell me something honest."

Niven erupted a little. "Why are you trying to make me cry? Because *you* can't?"

"Not at all," Jeep said. "I do need some whole answers though."

She looked at him with some defiance and then said, "Shoot."

"Did anyone leave the party with him?"

"Like who?"

"You can't answer a question with a question and call it being honest," Jeep said.

"Not that I saw. It was one of his Irish exits."

"Irish people make Irish exits. The main ingredients in Chambliss are England and Burgundy, France," Jeep said.

"You're being *such* an asshole."

"Johnny's back was all scratched up. The ME on the case won't sign off on an accidental death 'til someone explains how they got there."

"Like from sex?"

"Could well be."

"Well, it wasn't with me," she said.

"I didn't think it was or you would've told me by now. Or at least I hope you would've."

Jeep's manner and tone had none of the usual easy looseness he always tried to show her. She gave back some defiance.

"You going somewhere with this?"

"Right now, everywhere and nowhere. When Johnny had a beef with somebody he could play a very long game. He was still pulling the wings off an old lacrosse coach we had on account of the guy nicknamed him 'Careless' when he was a kid. One of quite a few examples I know of, and you probably know twice as many as me."

Her body language signaled acceptance; a heave of the shoulders, a shake of the head.

"Someone from your class he might've finally gotten into her pants? To get back at her for something, to get back at her husband for something?"

"And then what? She or he figured it out and killed him? That's some twisted imagination you got going," she said.

"I'm just trying to see if I can place someone with him before he went in the water. Maybe just went skinny-dipping with him. It's still plenty warm for it, you said so yourself. Late Saturday night it was still in the midseventies."

Niven seemed to have lost some of her armor. Jeep pivoted to a gentler tone.

"The window's closing. It could be there've been hands trying to close it since the morning after. Could be I just can't believe he simply decided to leave his high school reunion to take a moonlight swim all by his lonesome. The guy never did anything alone. He always needed an audience of at least one other person."

Niven took a pull from the bottle and offered it over. Jeep waved it away.

"The funeral's tomorrow. Once the body's in the ground a case tends to go cold and get colder every day after that. People just want to move on. And it could be the Nassau County guys got all there was to get when they ran their interviews. But I'd like to be sure, or as sure as I can be, that there's not information out there that I don't have."

"What do you want me to do?" Niven said, after a long moment.

"Ask around. Make up some bait and bait a hook. You've always been good at getting people to say what they're afraid to say 'cause they know you'll lighten the load."

"But you do it for a living, getting people to talk."

Jeep said, "Not these people. I'm a townie from here and they're from up there."

He'd pointed a thumb at the ground and then behind him.

She looked at him with an odd smile.

"What?" he said. "It's true."

"'You'll always be signing the guest book, you'll never be a member,'" she said.

Twenty years collapsed in an instant. Jeep's stomach flipped and he couldn't hide the hurt on his face, didn't even try. He tried to shake it off, failed. Niven looked away.

"I could be one cruel bitch back then. Pulling wings off flies for sport was something Johnny and I had in common. But I've never gotten so drunk I don't remember what I said. Especially to someone close."

"Why?" was all Jeep could manage.

"After umpteen years and a zillion dollars in shrinks? The consensus seems to be 'to see if they'll stick around and love you anyway.'"

Jeep wished he'd put down the whiskey after a couple of swigs. His head was full of static and his tongue was suddenly numb.

"You did have one of the all-time great lies, what you said I said."

"I don't remember."

"Oh yeah, you do." She stood up and stretched and lost her balance.

"Okaaaaaaaaay," she said, recovering.

Jeep stuffed the heel of the sandwich into the bag and squished it into a ball.

"I'll call you an Uber."

"I'm good to go, I've just been sitting too long."

"I said I'd call you an Uber." His tone flat and weary.

"I'll do it."

She reached for her phone and started poking at it.

"What's the house number?"

"Fourteen," he said.

She poked some more, then waited.

"Four minutes, how about that. Bayville be like the Meatpacking District all of a sudden."

She sat back down.

"I did talk to a lawyer. He didn't think the NDA had anything in it pertained to any investigation going on about Johnny," she said.

"Good."

She leaned into him a little.

"I'm gonna tell *you* something that's in it, though."

Jeep said, "Could it have anything to do with Saturday night?"

"No," she said. "But I think you should know—"

Jeep held up a hand, staying her.

"Then thank you, but totally not necessary."

But Niven never listened.

"Johnny fathered a child. I don't even know if it's a boy or a girl, he said that didn't matter. The kid is in that place in Chile where he went skiing in the summer, from some waitress or barmaid there he was snaking on the side."

Jeep just stared out at the water.

"He ever say anything to you?"

A phrase popped into his head. *Two can play at this game.*

Jeep finally turned to her. "No, never," he said.

Ten Years Earlier

Johnny had set one last trip to Portillo to ski during summer months to fulfill the requirements for his full inheritance.

I was a rookie NYPD officer stationed at the Seventeenth Precinct in Midtown East, one of the chosen few who patrolled the relatively safe streets of the tourist-heavy zones. It was rumored that those posts were traditionally awarded to young cops who could put a "friendly face" on the NYPD for the millions of visitors so vital to the city's economy. The CO put it more bluntly, saying I had a face "unencumbered by ethnic swarthiness."

Johnny had shamed me into coming with him with a not-untrue harangue about how barely traveled I was. Plus, he'd pressed, it's all paid for and only a three-day commitment. Truth was, it didn't take much shaming. We'd seen each other less and less, as he'd forecast, and the New York summer was especially brutal that year.

We spent one day at the lodge in Portillo, where Johnny got in the required day's runs. Sons of cops from Long Island generally don't grow up skiing, especially ones with a fear of heights, so I was happy to hang in my room in Portillo, Chile, South America, and marvel at the Andes from the window.

But by noon the second day we were in a suite at the Ritz-Carlton Santiago with early check-in because Johnny had a guy. By three that afternoon we were in the bleachers of a soccer field in the near suburbs, watching a game. Johnny passed me the binoculars he'd brought.

"Number nine, with the hair to his shoulders."

Number nine trotted off the field and turned toward us as he sat down on the bench.

I brought the glasses to my eyes and dialed the focus and saw why I was there.

The boy had his mother's light copper complexion, blushed from the cold and exertion. The boy had his father's features, right down to the high cheekbones and slightly ski-jump line of his nose. I put down the glasses.

"How old is he?"

"Eight."

"How long have you known?" I said.

"Well, since night before Thanksgiving sophomore year of college, when she showed up at Beagle's. You saw her, her name's Catalina. She had him the following May."

"What's his name?"

"Juan. Spanish for John."

"Do they call him 'Juanny'?"

Breaking the ice, as intended. He smiled.

"I don't think so."

"Doesn't have quite the same ring to it," I said.

He took the binoculars and pressed them to his eyes.

"He know you're here?"

"He doesn't know I exist," Johnny said.

"Who else does know who you are?"

"His mother and whoever she tells where the money comes from."

He lowered the glasses again.

"This is it. Thank you for coming with."

"What do you mean, *it*?" I said.

"Last time I'm coming down here to ski in Portillo. So, last time I'm going to see him."

"You can just send money and that's that?"

He looked at me, almost amused.

I said, "I'm sorry. I didn't mean it like that."

He said, "Don't be sorry, man. You've got it exactly right. What else would I be good for? Teach him to drive a stick?"

"You'd be good for a lot of things. Don't sell yourself short."

He said, "I'm not. I'm just being honest. The only thing I can do for him is also the best thing I can do for him, which is to provide more than a hotel waitress's salary can. All the other stuff, that's for some guy from around here. There's probably some dude he calls *padre* or whatever already and maybe for years now. As it should be."

An air horn sounded, signaling the end of the match. Juan and the other little victors hugged in a jumping huddle and then buried their goalie in a noisy scrum.

Johnny stood and stepped into the aisle and walked up the steps without a look back.

I followed behind him and saw him take off his sunglasses with one hand and reach for a bandanna from his coat pocket with the other and bring it around to his face.

Chapter Twelve

St. Luke's Episcopal Church in Lattingtown had an open field across the street for parking. The lot was about half full, mostly with high-end cars. Normally Jeep would post a single officer to direct traffic flow on and off the main road, but times being what they were Jeep called in reinforcements to post up on the perimeter. The last thing he needed was to have to explain to some mourner that the Mercedes he drove there in was probably on its way to the Port of Newark.

The only other time Jeep had been to an Episcopal service was for Johnny and Niven's wedding. The wedding did not have hymns as part of the ceremony. The funeral did have hymns, lots of them, and Jeep found out the hard way that Episcopalians sing every single verse of every single hymn. It was another in a run of unseasonably warm days; Indian summer was overstaying its welcome and the air in the church was moist and close despite the standing fans whirring on high, and his hangover wasn't helping matters one bit.

Jeep was serving as a pallbearer and so was seated on the aisle, by the casket, across from Pete and Gwen and their surviving grown children and a couple rows in front of Niven. The rector was holding forth about how "John's work here on earth was in service of his fellow man and he was a consummate pro" and how "John could light up the darkest night with his joie de vivre" and how "the Lord must have said to St. Peter, 'Heaven could use a guy like John,'" to a ripple of polite laughter.

After he finished, the rector called Niven up for a reading, which surprised Jeep some as growing up Catholic the mere acknowledgment of an ex-wife was a no-fly zone where the Church was concerned, much less giving one a role in the ceremony.

She took the rector's place at the lectern and adjusted the mic and opened a pocket missal to a ribbon-marked page.

"A reading from Ecclesiastes," she said.

Her voice rang loud and clear. "For everything there is a season, and a time for every matter under heaven," she began.

She put some mustard on a couple of the greatest hits, especially "a time to love, and a time to hate" and "a time to tear and a time to mend." She closed the missal as the rector stood to resume his emcee-ing duties. But she stayed at the lectern and turned and spoke to him directly, cordially.

"If I may, Rector Sturdevant? He was never called 'John,' he's always been 'Johnny.' I'm sure they didn't speak of *John* Carson or *Jim* Buffett at those guys' funerals. That 'eee' ending is something they clearly liked or they would've done something about it early on. So, it's *Johnny*. Thank you."

She returned to her pew amid some whispering and some surprised looks from the assembled. Jeep caught her eye and she slid him a split-second expression asking *Amiright?* He smiled and nodded to her.

The rector finally wrapped it up and the two pros from the funeral home signaled silently to the other four pallbearers, including Jeep, to take up their positions.

The rector shot the organist a look like she was late to her cue. But the organist was looking at another young woman, who was coming up the side aisle with a fiddle and a bow.

The crowd stirred. Jeep thought to himself, it can't be.

The two women began to play an intro, tossing looks at each other, getting in sync.

The fiddle was a brilliant stroke, giving the arrangement a timeless, rural aspect. When the organist began to sing in her soaring soprano it was as if she'd called up the very first moment she realized she had a voice and could move people with it.

Jeep stole a look at Gwen, who was looking over Pete's shoulder as he leaned in and whispered his fierce objection.

Gwen was looking right at Jeep. Her expression, it struck him, carried an unmistakable challenge: bring me the truth, whatever it is, whatever it takes.

The soprano filled the rafters as she reached the first chorus: "My ride's here, my ride's here . . ."

They rolled the coffin slowly down the aisle.

Jeep started to cry, and couldn't hold back. And he didn't just cry, he wept.

The post-internment reception was held at the Two Trees Club's beach outpost on Wolf Point. It had a swimming pool and rows of cabanas and a bar and a dining pavilion and patio overlooking the beach and the Sound. What it did not have, despite annual pleas by younger members, was air conditioning. Until the last of the Greatest and the Boomer generations died off, the refreshing sea breezes were all a right-minded person could need.

But the air was still hot and humid and the tide was slack with an oily sheen. Jeep had spent most of the evening avoiding Pete and Gwen, both when together and apart; he couldn't see himself pleading "don't kill the messenger" to Pete about the Warren Zevon song and felt uncertain about Gwen's motives in defying her husband. The clear challenge he felt in the church had given way to uncertainty; she could just have been sticking it to Pete for sport or payback. And even if he did understand her correctly, he still didn't have any alternative theory to the conventional wisdom of "accidental."

Jeep didn't have to stay for the duration but he couldn't be among the first to leave, per Niven's rules of civility. So he walked around back with a beer in hand, taking care to look to be grieving solo should anyone be clocking him.

Jeep stepped up onto the seawall and watched a cherry red cigarette boat heading east at full throttle and wondered whether there were speed limits on the open water. He figured if there were, he'd know, but cut himself a break if he'd missed cop class that day.

He watched as the boat shrank to a speck. A gull with a clam in its beak skidded to a hover and dropped the clam from on high to smash on the Bayville beach parking lot asphalt. Jeep heard a faint alarm go off in his head.

The Bayville public beach parking lot ended at a two-track that connected with the east side of the Two Trees Beach Club parking area, a level knoll of lawn used for overflow from the paved lot. The path served as a fire access road to the club; the only other way in was Wolf Lane with its one-car width and restricted-weight rickety wooden bridge. But times were different now what with Google Earth maps and endlessly inventive young criminals and the path could double-duty as the red carpet to a silver platter of Audis, Bentleys, Beemers, Porsches and Mercs whose owners wouldn't think to lock up as it was private parking for a private club, and membership had its privileges.

He jogged over and reached for his radio from his Tahoe and keyed it. Jackson answered.

"It's Chief. Get Diaz and post up one of you at the west-end Bayville Beach lot and the other at the head of Wolf Lane."

"We talking speed traps?"

"No. The car thieves. Probably nothing but I'm at a thing at the Beach Club and I just had a flash."

"Copy that. Ten-four."

Jeep reached for his off-duty SIG Sauer P365 and his shield chain from the console bin and holstered the gun in his waistband and slipped the chain over his head and grabbed the radio.

He walked up the knoll and found a vantage point on a boulder at the edge of the scrub oak and checked the coast. At one end of his field of vision was the entrance to the club and at the other was the exit of the Bayville beach path. There was no lighting in the lot save for the final few watts of sunset.

Two couples came down the steps and the walkway out from the dining pavilion. A car alarm chirped, disarming, and the head-and-tail-lights of a 7 Series BMW lit up. Jeep silently complimented the owner on his vigilance and thanked Jackson for the email blasts to the communities. In ninety percent of car thefts in the area, the keys were in the unlocked cars and so the side-view mirrors were extended like open arms to thieves.

The couples shook and hugged their farewells by the Beemer for a good couple minutes and then that couple boarded, him helping a clearly overserved her into the passenger seat.

The other couple started toward the rear of the lot closer to the beach. The woman took the man's hand as they walked.

Jeep turned his attention back to where the two-track met the grassy knoll. Nothing to see here.

The BMW backed out and rolled south toward the wooden bridge over the tidal marsh on Wolf Lane.

The man and the woman stopped and kissed and hugged each other.

The BMW braked on the bridge. Jeep stood up. What ran through his mind was, a thief waiting behind the car, slipping in back when the doors chirped open.

Jeep ran with that, for about ten yards.

When he saw the woman lurch out of the car, lean over the bridge rail, and vomit.

A man's shout and a woman's scream turned him back around. Jeep got the news flash: He was watching for someone who was, in fact, watching him. As an Aston Martin DBX barked to life.

The couple yelled "stop" and "help"; the Aston shot back in reverse out of the parking slot.

Jeep keyed the radio, running full tilt toward the back of the lot.

"Ten-ten all units Wolf Lane terminus lot!"

His right knee howled at him but he accelerated as the Aston swung around pointed right at him, the headlights blinding him.

He rolled the radio to the grass and reached for his shield and held it out.

"POLICE! STOP!"

The Aston shot forward. Jeep fell to one knee and grabbed the gun from his waistband and raised it.

The Aston skidded to a stop. Jeep stood back up and held the gun level.

"STEP OUT OF THE VEHICLE!"

Either the thief didn't understand English or, more likely, just started laughing as he floored it in reverse. Jeep launched in pursuit and told his knee to shut the fuck up. The Aston skidded to a stop again and the driver cut the wheel and arced toward the rise of the knoll.

Jeep lunged and got a hand on the passenger-side door handle and pulled it open. There were two of them, a pilot and a wingman, both in hoodies.

The driver accelerated and his wingman tried to pull the door shut but Jeep hung on. The driver braked hard and then floored it again, trying to shake Jeep off. But in the split second of stasis Jeep had managed to reach in and get purchase on the wingman's hoodie, and the Aston's acceleration was a blessing now as the g-force slid the wingman right into Jeep's embrace. They rolled down the knoll as the Aston lurched across the grass and onto the two-track leading out.

Jeep jerked the wingman's arms behind his back and reached his handcuffs and got him shackled and ran a speed-frisk that turned up empty.

"CAN I GET A HAND?!" he yelled out.

The assembled had gathered on the steps and the walkway. It was Niven who ran out.

"Are you all right?!"

"Radio's in the grass over there." He jerked his head. "Go!"

She went. The wingman swore in Spanish. Jeep jerked his wrists farther up toward his shoulder blades. The wingman yelped but stopped swearing.

Jeep saw the Aston's owner and his wife holding each other by the pool fence twenty yards away.

"Anybody hurt?" he called over.

"We're okay," the man said.

Niven brought the radio.

Jeep dropped his good knee in the small of the wingman's back and keyed the radio.

"All units ten-fourteen Aston Martin SUV last seen headed Bayville Beach parking lot; all units ten-seventy-eight Wolf Lane terminus lot and call a bus, over."

Immediately the responses started crackling as the sirens grew closer.

The families and guests gathered at a perimeter, in shock. Niven peppered Jeep with questions, but they sounded to him like they were coming from underwater. The responses over the radio blurred into an indistinct squawk and rumble. His right knee stabbed him a good one as he stood up and hauled the wingman to his feet and marched him to the Tahoe and Mirandized him in Spanish as two units trundled over the bridge and pulled up hot.

Chapter Thirteen

Jeep had Bondurant ride with him to process the wingman at the Nassau PD second squad over in Westbury. With the kid secured in the back they passed the time on the ride by making up a wish list of miracles that would burden the kid with something more than a DAT, a desk appearance ticket to appear in court three or four weeks later. The chances of the kid actually showing up were somewhere between "take a miracle" and "less than zero."

"Child porn on his phone," Jeep said.

"We don't got a warrant for his phone plus, not for nothing, he's practically a child himself," Bondurant said.

"His ID's on a photo or a screenshot in the gallery, so they *have* to check it, no warrant necessary."

"Ninety-nine-point-nine percent it's a burner phone and they don't keep photo galleries on 'em. So, nope."

"They run his prints and there's an outstanding warrant."

"Him being in the system is about same odds it's not a burner phone."

They could have done this all the way to Montauk but they turned off Jericho Turnpike into the second squad.

• • •

A Detective Simpson had caught processing duties that night and Jeep could tell he was a pro at handling cops who were handling perps who were about to be set scot free by the way he kept it firm but sympathetic.

"Did he assault you in any way?"

"He rolled out of a moving Aston Martin and onto my person," Jeep tried.

"You said you pulled him out," Simpson said.

"I pulled him out of the car where he was in commission of a crime."

"Acting in concert," Simpson corrected.

"Now you're really splitting hairs," Jeep said.

Simpson was a large Black man in his fifties and had the kind of world-weary manner that was clearly earned, not posed, and broadcast *seen it, heard it, fuck it.*

"I'm just trying to keep both of us from getting jammed up over trumping some shit to hold a seventeen-year-old kid for boosting a car. Ain't worth it."

"It is to me."

Simpson raised his caterpillar eyebrows as high as they would go.

"No, it is not. You know the drill and I know the drill. No warrants on him so just a Desk Appearance ticket. D-A-T, d-d-d-dat's all, folks."

Jeep walked over to Bondurant, who was sitting next to their hand-cuffed ex-prisoner.

"Same as it ever was," he said to Bondurant as he gestured for the wingman, whose name turned up as Rodrigo, to stand and turn around. He unlocked the cuffs and pocketed them.

The kid sat back down, rubbing his wrists. Jeep squared off in front of him, bending over with his hands on his knees like an old-timey football lineman.

"Hey, Rodrigo. Help me help you."

Simpson called over, warning, "Chief Mullane? Uh-uh. He's been processed and released."

The kid looked at Jeep with a feral sulk and slipped his phone out of his jeans and keyed it on and started texting.

On the way back Jeep and Bondi bitched awhile about bail reform and politicians and judges and the worldwide famine of common sense but it was an old song and they were both sick of it so they changed the station to silence.

After a while the radio crackled. Jackson on the frequency, words all run together.

"Chief I've got a DWI stopped on Northern Boulevard West just past 106 and I need you to come here right now and that's all I got for over the radio so *over*."

Jeep and Bondi traded puzzled looks and Jeep hit the switches and lit up the overhanging trees in blue strobes and floored it.

Detective Arbogast was planted against the door of his black Cadillac CTS-V with his head down and his back to the street so as to avoid any chance recognition from a looky-loo slowing down for a gawk.

Jeep and Bondurant conferred with Jackson about twenty yards over.

"Was he abusive in any way?" Jeep asked.

"I think he would've been if I refused to call you but no."

"The woman with him?"

The woman with him was sitting in the passenger seat of the Cadillac with the dome light still on, texting on her phone.

"No, fully cooperative."

"But he was driving?" Jeep said.

"Blew a point-one-five so DWI and one drink short of Aggravated."

"Walk with me," Jeep said.

The three of them went over to Arbogast's Cadillac. Jeep patted air by the hood, signaling the two to wait there. He went around and set his ass on the car next to Arbogast.

"You married, Detective?"

"Yeah."

"To the lady in the front seat?"

"You know that's a no."

Arbogast paying Jeep the respect that Jeep, as an observant cop, would recognize her as the waitress from the Thai restaurant.

"Your wife out of town?"

"No. She's home."

"She put up with your bullshit all these years, still loves you anyway?"

Of course, he didn't answer. He flashed some anger but held his tongue.

"Where you live?"

"Split Rock Road in Syosset."

No slurred words, no emotional outbursts or naked pleading, no nothing. Even his hair was perfect. A pro like Arbogast could finish the whole bottle and still keep his cop cool.

"Okay, here's how this can go. I drive you home, walk you to the door, hand you off all buddy-buddy to the missus, tell her we met for a bite and I'm a killjoy and erred on the side of caution after you had that third Scotch. You with me?"

Arbogast finally looked at Jeep, suspicion in his eyes.

"Why?" he said.

"Not yet. We're gonna lock your car in the Greek church lot over there, you get it in the morning. We do this right, your squad don't know, CO don't know, HQ don't know, the wife don't know. *Nobody* has to know you were driving her to the Won't-Tell Motel blowing a point-one-five."

Arbogast took a moment, digesting.

"Why?" he asked again.

"My old man, he was an NYPD detective, I tell you that? Died from poisons he breathed working at Ground Zero, I tell you that? Anyways, he always said, 'You can never have enough favors out on the street.' Now, he meant with skells and dirtbags and potential CIs of course. But I think it goes for other cops sometimes, too. Like say, you. Do 'em a favor, you get the chance."

This was where even a pro like Arbogast could feel compromised by the booze, trying to follow Jeep's line of thought. But Arbogast took a stab at it.

"What the fuck favor could I do for you?" he said.

"Well, say you got a warrant and dumped my friend's phone, maybe dipped a toe in the theory that maybe it wasn't purely *accidental*. You'd have who called him, who he called, what time, how long, what cell towers it pinged off of. So there's at least that. Some other baskets of goodies you found, not you maybe, maybe Slocum, he seems like a pain-in-the-ass go-getter. Maybe, maybe not. But Detective, I've still got bad dreams. About are there questions buried in that coffin six feet under with my old friend. About how'd the scratches on his back get there, about where's his watch."

Jeep thought he saw a little flinch, those last two.

"That keeps me tossing and turning and I can't find a cool side of the pillow. And I usually sleep like a baby and wake up all *refreshed*, and I miss that."

Jeep just waited him out, watching him out of the corner of his eye. Thunder cracked in the distance and the leaves started swishing in a sudden breeze like predicting a break in the heat.

"What about the girl?" he said.

"The girl calls an Uber. I'm not a fucking chauffeur."

When Jeep got home he saw that Niven had gone four for four; the G-Wagen was parked out front. Jeep thought maybe he should get a sign with her name and that red tow-truck icon on it but he was in no mood for even his own jokes. That night it was Jeep who felt like the cartoon character; he was Deputy Dawg, but instead of funny little varmints and critters making a fool of him he had fearless car thieves with brass balls.

The rain was coming down sideways; Jeep cleared his head and realized (a) Niven wouldn't be out back in this and (b) there were lights on in his house and he always locked up his house.

She was sitting on the couch with a beer and a bag of microwaved popcorn watching some show with British accents.

"Honey, you're home!" she said.

"What'd you, break in?"

Clearly, he wasn't playing. She aimed the remote and muted the TV.

"No. The other night I noticed you had one of those little gray fake rocks from back in the last century that had a compartment for a spare key. I thought 'nah' but tried it anyway and lo and behold."

Jeep's dad had bought one at the True Value and thought it was pretty clever and set it among the shells and driftwood out by the back deck sometime in the midnineties. No one had ever found it and used it to gain entry until that night.

"I took a bunch of food from the reception and put it in your fridge. Which is why I 'broke in.' You're welcome."

He went in the kitchen and opened the refrigerator and got a beer and a tin plate of tomato-mozzarella-basil stacks and a bag of frozen corn from the freezer and went back to her.

"I just can't tonight, okay?"

He gulped down a third of the beer and tied the frozen corn to his bad knee with a napkin. He ate with his hands.

"Okay. But I didn't come by just to bother you."

"You don't bother me. It's just been a string of long bad days."

"I know. And you were very brave tonight, if that's okay to say."

"But there's still an Aston Martin gone missing on my watch."

"But you caught one of them."

"Who's probably out partying in the city somewhere or already on a flight back to Bogotá or wherever."

"Wait, *what*?"

He looked at her, flat out of gas.

"A fucked-up story for another time."

His look like, *final*. She got it and took it graciously. She rolled up the top of the popcorn bag, sealing it.

"Before I go: why I came? You remember Lisbet Woodard?"

"Yeah, she was at the wake."

"She was at the reunion, too. And she was out back behind some bushes and she heard Johnny on a phone call."

"Behind some bushes, eavesdropping?"

"No, she just happened to be out there."

"Uh-huh. And did she share this with the Nassau detectives?"

"No."

Jeep losing patience. "No, because?"

"Because she was out there behind some bushes diddling Juliet Haskell."

Jeep needed a moment, as he often did when trying to follow a Niven story.

"They're both married with kids but apparently they've had some *Brokeback Mountain* thing going on since the last reunion," she said. "Can't say I'm shocked, they always gave off this whole field-hockey-meets-Avril-Lavigne vibe, plus they both went to Brown."

Jeep wasn't sure what any of that meant so he just stayed the course.

"She told you this in what context?" he said.

"You said I was good at getting people to talk and that I lightened their load. So I called around and when I reached Lisbet she spilled about her and Juliet hearing Johnny on the phone."

"Did she say what she overheard?"

"A little. But she's willing to talk to you. Neither she nor Juliet told the Nassau detectives 'cause they didn't trust them not to blab it all over town. She said they trust you."

"She say why?"

"She didn't need to. Everybody trusts you."

She got up and put the popcorn and the empty beer bottle in the kitchen.

"Did you feel any better after you finally cried?"

Jeep didn't really have a true answer.

"I guess."

She came back in.

"You *guess*? After a display like that?"

"It wasn't a *display*. Just like, everything got the better of me, all at once."

She looked at him, dubious.

He said, "You cry when you feel sad or you're hurt. It doesn't make the *why* of it go away. So how it would make you feel better, I never got that."

She thought about that for a moment, shrugged it off.

"When are you back to work?" he said.

"Ooooh. *Someone's* overstayed her welcome."

"No, I just meant . . ." He broke off.

"My parents leave tomorrow for Hilton Head, back on Monday, so I said I'd house-sit. Plus, Edwin from work took three whole weeks after his husband died so I figure an ex-wife widow gets a week, easy."

He said, "Would Lisbet be more comfortable if you were there?"

She said, "Everyone's more comfortable if I'm there. Except you."

As she passed by on her way to the door she bent down and kissed the top of his head.

"Remember what Johnny'd say? 'Why beat yourself up, the world does it for you.'"

Nine Years Earlier

I was ten minutes early but the weather in New York City that December evening had the kind of cold wet bite that would drive a sled dog to claw at the kitchen door.

The law offices of Hutchinson and Aames took up a whole high floor of a landmark skyscraper just east of Grand Central Terminal. I was meeting Johnny there before a Rangers game at the Garden. I'd offered to just meet him at the street-level bar like a normal person but Johnny insisted because the lounge at the firm had a library of every *National Geographic* magazine dating from 1919, when the firm was founded, and he thought I should see it. The lounge also had a small open whiskey bar where none of the Scotch was younger than twenty years old, and Johnny always made it a point to have a couple because: "You add up the fees over all the years, it's easily a million dollars a drink." I poured a couple fingers of Macallan 25 and pulled the August 1927 issue and sat in a fat leather chair and settled in to enjoy the wait.

Johnny and I had hung out a grand total of nine days that year, including the trip to Chile. I knew this because Niven had counted them up on her social calendar, which is what she called the old-school

Filofaxes stuffed with ticket stubs and boarding passes and restaurant matchbooks where she'd recorded her extracurricular life since the sixth grade. She had exhaustively cataloged feuds, obsessions, goals, crushes, favors granted and received, diet and exercise regimens, pecking orders and sexual acts in a code she claimed she'd cribbed from World War II British Secret Service records. I doubted that but every couple of years she'd challenge me to decipher a page or two and I never once got traction.

The days we were together that year were spent out on the North Shore on weekends I got off. I'd split my time between having breakfast with my mom and doing chores around her house for the days and hanging with Johnny and Niven and the various single females she'd match me up with as "blond dates" for the nights. My actual girlfriend that summer was a redheaded actress from an Indiana factory town who tended bar at Balthazar on weekends and who would have spent the whole time with that tribe just looking at me cross-eyed.

I enjoyed the doubles tennis and the kayak trips and the poolside lunches and pretended to enjoy the dinner parties and the dinner-dances and the after-parties. By August I begged off the invitations; I was studying for the Sergeant's Exam and hadn't had to hit the books like that since college. That was my excuse, anyway.

The truth was a little more complicated. I had a tribe of my own by then; the cops from my house, the girls from the bars and the gym, the motley crew I played pickup lax with in the parks on the East River by the FDR.

Johnny and Niven and I could always pick up right where we left off and it felt like wherever we were together was our treehouse or diner booth or back row. But I'd started to feel isolated and self-conscious as their circle seemed to be in a rush to middle age; in my city life I was in a mostly pleasurable rut of the daily this and the nightly that, with a fair share of life's rich pageant thrown in. But out there I felt more and more like my fly was open or my armpits had sweaty crescent moons even though I knew it wasn't so. And the war stories that killed in the precinct locker room or at the bars were mostly met with a kind of polite incredulity on the tennis courts or in the club dining rooms.

Johnny careened in ten minutes late and hooked his down vest on the rack and rubbed off the cold as the receptionist stood up.

"They're waiting for you, Mr. Chambliss."

"Betsy, you cut your hair!" Johnny said.

"I did," she said.

"I swear to God, I first walked in, I thought they'd replaced you with Jennifer Aniston!"

Betsy looked nothing like Jennifer Aniston and likely knew it but blushed anyway.

"I'm so glad you approve."

She came out around the desk as Johnny poured a couple inches of whiskey into a tumbler and said to me, "Fifteen minutes, tops. Try the Lagavulin."

He followed her through the mahogany doors to the inner sanctums. I turned to an article about migration in the Masai Mara.

Ninety seconds later he was back. He held the door open and pointed at me.

"I need you."

The conference room had bottle-green walls hung with oil portraits of, I guessed, partners from over the years. Pete Chambliss stood up from the table, clearly surprised to see me.

"Jeep," he said. He frowned at Johnny.

"Hi, Mr. Chambliss."

I shook his offered hand.

Johnny said to him, "I don't know why you're here or what's going on but I figure I deserve counsel, too."

"Jeep's a police officer, not an attorney."

"He's always been good counsel to me, though. So let's get started, we've got Rangers tickets."

I was introduced to the two other men in the room, a Bill Logan and a Perry Duke, both trust and estate attorneys, both straight out of Pete's gene pool, from the looks of them. We all sat down to place settings of yellow legal pads and ballpoint pens in perfect alignment.

Pete said to Johnny, "Does Jeep know about the bastard?"

Johnny took a deep breath and kept a grip, barely. Bill and Perry, flanking Pete, muttered cautiously under their breaths.

"I'm not gonna tiptoe," Pete said to them.

"Yes, he does," Johnny said.

Perry grabbed the wheel.

"Have you had a paternity test done?"

"No. But the kid is mine."

"And you know this, how?"

"I've seen him. A father can tell, I guess." Johnny aimed over at Pete, sarcastic, "Ain't that right, Pop? Help me out here?"

Pete just scribbled on his legal pad. Bill picked up the ball.

"The firm's concern, your *father's* concern, is the exposure the family's wealth and reputation faces. Is the mother making demands?"

"No. None," Johnny said.

"So the scheduled five thousand a month going to her in Santiago is purely of your own volition."

"Yes."

Johnny looked at his father again.

"How'd you find out?"

"We followed the money."

"You put a detective on your own son?"

Pete looked to his attorneys to do their jobs. Perry cleared his throat.

"Johnny, we needed to be sure that there wasn't anything illegal going on."

"And now you know, right?"

"The money's not the issue here. There's still the matter of exposure." Perry looked over at Bill like, *your turn*.

"The payments could serve as a de facto admission of paternity, in court."

"I am the father. That's the fact-o," Johnny said.

"And open us up to lawsuits, to inheritance claims, any number—"

"—of bullshit grabs some Santiago ambulance chaser could think up," Pete cut in.

"You got any evidence of that?" Johnny said.

"I've walked this earth for sixty-six years. I've got all the evidence I need."

He slid looks to Bill and Perry.

"Has the mother contacted you recently?" Perry said.

"No. Not in years. Why?"

Both Bill and Perry looked to Pete, who nodded.

"The automatic wire transfer has been terminated," Bill said. "As of last week."

"You can't do that," Johnny said.

"We can and we did, as trustees," Pete said. Then, to Perry, "Let's move this along. They have a Rangers game and I have a dinner."

Bill reached for two documents, one about an inch thick and bound, the other a couple of sheets and stapled. He slid them across the table to Johnny.

"The document on your right confirms that on January first another thirty-three percent of the trust is released into your accounts, as scheduled. It has a rider for you to sign that you will not attempt to make any further payments to a Ms. Catalina Soto of Santiago, Chile—"

"Or anywhere else," Pete interjected.

"—for any purposes whatsoever including but not limited to expenses incurred or projected for her son Juan."

If Johnny ever needed a guy, it was now. And all he had was me.

"The other document is an acknowledgment and acceptance that, should you decline to endorse the rider to the first document, you renounce all claims to the trust, its capital and its income, in perpetuity."

All he had was me, and there wasn't a damn thing I could do, as a friend or as a cop. The silence lasted seconds you'd swear were minutes.

Pete finally broke it, in a soft voice.

"Johnny, you're my son and I love you and years from now you will—"

"Please stop," Johnny said, cutting him off.

Johnny picked up the pen and pulled the legal pad closer and wrote down a name. The first name was "Diana," I couldn't make out the last. He tore off the sheet and folded it and pushed it across the table to his father.

Pete held his gaze and then picked it up and opened it. He looked crushed, and about as close to bursting into tears as a man like him ever got. He folded the paper closed.

"She knows about her," he said.

Johnny scribbled another name, ripped the sheet, folded it and pushed it over. Pete looked at it.

"About her, too." You could barely hear him, and Perry poured and passed a glass of water.

Johnny did tear up, but pressed his hands to his face like he could push the tears back into his eyes.

He reached the two-sheet document renouncing his claim and slid it toward him and flipped to the second page where there was a red arrow sticker by a line at the bottom and he signed it and pushed it away.

"Jeep, our work here is done," he said, with more bravado than I thought would be possible. He dropped the pen on the table with a flourish and stood up and headed for the door and I followed after.

We'd walked a couple of blocks before he said anything and all he said was, "Sometimes you gotta kick your *own* ass."

I asked some money questions and got non-answers except to the last one.

"Did you at least save something?" I asked.

"Hopefully, a shred of dignity."

The seats were on the glass so we saw the smashmouth game up close. The Rangers beat the Boston Bruins 4–3 in a shoot-out. I bought all the beers.

Chapter Fourteen

Like Jeep, Lisbet Woodard had migrated back to the village she was raised in. Unlike Jeep, her return had been hardwired from the beginning, as it was for many of her classmates and club-mates. It could seem as if there was DNA in their genetic map that routed them from Shelter Rock or St. Somebody's to Ivy League or NESCAC college to New York or Boston and then back to the North Shore by age thirty with spouse and baby in tow. The North Shore would always be Home, and in Lisbet's case, had been for generations. There was a Woodard Nature Preserve, a Woodard Recreation Center, and Woodard Square, a mixed-use office complex on Woodard Road.

"Just to be clear, I didn't hear all of it, he was kind of pacing toward and away from where I was," Lisbet said. "And it's not like I wrote it down."

"Of course," Jeep said.

They were sitting at a wrought-iron-and-glass dining table under an ivied pergola out back of Niven's parents' home. The house itself was the kind of elegant brick-and-shingle 1930s Colonial whose herringbone floors and copper gutters prompted people to say, "They sure don't build 'em like this anymore."

"Plus you're not under oath or anything," Niven said.

Jeep slid her a look.

"That's true. It's technically not my investigation, but it occurred in my jurisdiction, and I'd appreciate anything you're certain you remember."

Lisbet was just pretty enough to be labeled attractive in those parts and wore the fit-mom uniform of Lululemons, Barbour, and chronic cheeriness.

"I'm pretty sure he took the call rather than made it."

"What makes you say that?"

"Juliet and I had one eye on the French doors to the patio, you know, just so's not to be surprised if someone wandered out."

"And saw you, what, smoking a joint?" Jeep said.

Niven tossed him a look; he didn't field it.

"You'd be surprised what still gets people talking around here," Lisbet said, looking right at him.

He smiled and nodded. She returned it. He'd passed a test.

"Anyway, I say that because he kind of hurried outside and then put the phone to his ear like he'd already picked up."

"Good observation, thank you," Jeep said.

"So then he starts walking around like in a circle, mostly listening, then when he talked it'd be like, short, like yes or no almost. Not that I could hear everything 'cause the circle would go away from us and then back toward us. So if you think of it like we're in the stands at a car race and he's a car, we'd have a clear view for a few seconds a lap."

"Got it."

"So it seemed to me that he was trying to end the call, you know, like to get back to the party. But it must have been important for him to take the call in the first place plus come outside for privacy, right?"

"Lisbet, have you ever considered a career as an ace detective?"

Which made her laugh and made Jeep wonder about a couple of things, first and foremost of which was, if Lisbet and Juliet were busy up each other's skirts 'cause the heart wants what it wants, what's with all the attention to detail of a guy taking a phone call?

"Lisbet, just a sec so I'm clear. You said you smoked a joint, yes?"

"Yes."

"Where you going with this?" Niven said.

"I'm just saying, if Lisbet was baked, it may have affected her memory of what he said."

Niven shot Jeep a look; Lisbet blushed.

"Okay, full disclosure?" she said. "I didn't inhale, weed makes me get all paranoid."

So, truth with a side of fibs. As truth was often served.

Lisbet continued, "Anyways, this is the important part. He's maybe twenty feet from us and he stops walking the circle, stands still, he's in earshot. He goes, 'Where are you?' He listens. He goes, 'Okay, turn your back to the water and tell me what you see.' He listens some more, going 'uh-huh, uh-huh.' Then he says, 'I know right where you are. Sit tight, I'll be there as soon as I can.' Then he ended the call and went back inside."

Jeep's mind raced. He tried to tear her story down to the studs.

Someone called Johnny, had his cell number. Someone not from around here, couldn't give his or her location. The caller's location was by the water. Johnny said he'd meet him or her but did not immediately go to meet him or her.

"About what time was this?"

"About ten thirty."

"Did you see Johnny again?"

"No. We decided to skip the long goodbyes and just split. But I knew Johnny drove one of those old Land Rovers, my husband always points it out in town like, hint, hint, 'I've got a birthday coming up.' It was gone when we left."

Jeep had a hastily scheduled noon meeting with Donahue and the other three mayors at the Big Stick, a popular Teddy Roosevelt–themed pub in Oyster Bay. As he said his goodbyes to Lisbet and Niven his phone buzzed with a text that the venue had been changed to the western Bayville beach parking lot, which bode badly on two levels. One, it was still partially taped off as a crime scene from last night's debacle and so a visceral reminder of his shortcomings as a crime stopper, and two, if a meeting was moved from a public place to an isolated one it usually meant, in movies and in life, that you were about to get whacked in one way or another.

Jeep took the left off the Bayville road and passed the empty parking-pass checkpoint kiosk and drove toward the four mayors, who were milling by their cars near the back end.

He parked twenty yards away and got out and walked slowly toward them.

Throw in a couple of tumbleweeds, some frightened townsfolk and a lone barking dog and it was all Donahue could have hoped for: *High Noon*.

"Afternoon, Mayors," Jeep said.

Mayors Chaz Scarborough, Maisie Coffin and Mark LaSalle came right back with friendly, if muted, greetings. Donahue went last.

"Chief Mullane, thanks for coming out."

"We're still waiting on the full account but the NYPD plate readers got nothing, they must've switched the tags before the Queens line. An accomplice was taken into custody and booked by me personally and given a desk appearance ticket."

"A *ticket*?"

Donahue putting on a little show, turning to the others so all could see the incredulous expression on his face.

"Yes, Mayors. A summons to appear in court. A round of applause please for New York State Senate 2019-S2101A."

Maisie said, "It's really that bad?"

"Not if you're a criminal," Jeep said. "They *Heart* New York."

Jeep looked at Donahue.

"Let's get to it, Mr. Mayor. I'm assuming it's you called this meeting?" Jeep tried for affable, failed.

Chaz Scarborough said, "We all called it, Chief. We're all on the same page here."

Chaz Scarborough was the youngest of the four mayors. He was also the youngest governor on the board at Two Trees and the youngest partner at his private equity firm. He was also younger than Jeep by four years, which made Jeep feel old for the first real time.

Donahue actually widened his stance and crossed his arms.

"We had some face time with the PC down at One Law this morning."

Which translated as they'd met with Rick Knight, the county's police commissioner, at headquarters at One Law Enforcement Way in Garden City. Nobody called it One Law except Donahue, and Jeep wondered if even a pro like Knight managed to keep a straight face with him.

"The PC agreed with me that these banditos are just way too much for the local PDs up here. I said we need the cavalry and he's agreed to send the cavalry."

The other three, suddenly absent from the conversation in Donahue's recounting, inspected the tips of their shoes.

"So Commissioner Knight said he'd pull manpower from Hempstead and Uniondale and give the gangs and the dope dealers a break while he tackled the wave of citizens leaving their cars unlocked up on the Gold Coast?" Jeep's voice rose steadily right up to the "Gold Coast."

Scarborough and LaSalle tried to disappear, failed. Maisie Coffin fought back a smile and mostly succeeded. Donahue stared Jeep down. Jeep played along. Donahue finally spoke, measured, large and in charge.

"It was an initial strategy meeting. Manpower allocation figures are TBD."

Jeep said, "Which brings us to the second item on our agenda, no?"

All four mayors looked a little puzzled.

Donahue said, "Our agenda or your agenda?"

Jeep said, "Well, ours, I guess. The matter of my replacement concerns all of us."

Maisie Coffin showed her hand. "Please don't quit, Chief." No one seconded her motion.

"I'm not, Maisie, and thank you. But the next stop on *this* train is where I get thrown off. So, two things before we get there. My contract guarantees a whole year's salary, plus health, no matter what. Unless someone thinks they've got me on dereliction of duty, which they don't, by any stretch of the definition."

Mark LaSalle picked up that gauntlet. Mark controlled family-legacy seats on the New York Stock and Chicago Mercantile Exchanges and considered himself an "averages" guy.

"Apples and oranges, Chief. That decision wouldn't be made on a deficit cost basis. Just for the record."

Jeep's forehead crawled with little beads of flop sweat. He pressed on.

"Folks, cops don't pitch no-hitters. We work hard to get the occasional strike or pop fly in a game where we're always behind and the bases are always loaded, no outs, and the ninth inning never comes. So thank you for meeting with me, but if you'll excuse me I should get back to work."

But Jeep stayed just long enough to see that they were all deeply unmoved. Just long enough to remember that he was from down here and they were from up there. Just long enough to realize that were he in their shoes, he'd probably be looking at himself with the same exasperation. And just long enough to agree that they could do whatever they wanted with him or to him; he served at their pleasure, as the saying goes.

Jeep turned away and walked to his vehicle. If he was a cartoon character just then he was Bugs Bunny's nemesis Yosemite Sam after Bugs pulled Sam's big hat down over his whole body and he teetered around blind with just his little boots showing under the brim of the hat. Worse, the whole point of his dad's mind game was to level your playing field by imagining other people as the cartoon characters, not yourself.

Jeep got in and hit the lights and sirens and laid down six feet of rubber on the way out, the only move he could think of.

Upon his return, Jeep was informed by Corporal Jackson that the Nassau County Police Commissioner's office had called with a request for Chief Mullane to drop by as soon as humanly fucking possible. Not in those words exactly, but that was the gist she got when she answered the phone while their administrative assistant Serena pumped her breast milk in the ladies' room.

"What up, you think?" Jackson said, her eyes on Jeep like a card sharp watching for a tell.

"Maybe he wants to give me a medal for the action last night," Jeep said.

She brightened. "You think?"

"Could be. The Bozo Award for Pointless Heroics in Service of a DAT."

She dimmed. "What did the Mayors want?"

He just shook his head.

"Mind driving me? I don't trust myself behind the wheel right now."

"Sure. You eat? We could stop on the way."

"I ate with the Mayors. I had the shit special."

She had that face on that he both loved and hated. A cop should never look at her CO with pity or concern for his mental well-being. On the other hand, it's always nice to know someone cares.

Chapter Fifteen

The new Nassau Police Department Headquarters was a modern campus carved out of vacant acreage abutting the community college. It featured a command center with an IMAX-size screen split into dozens of feeds ranging from doorbell cameras to helicopter surveillance and, in an adjoining lot, a scale mock-up of a typical Long Island village center for tactical training exercises. All it lacked was an obstacle course to prepare recruits for the rigors of a broken legal system.

"And we never had this meeting," Commissioner Knight offered as a greeting after they shook hands. In his midforties, he had the shorn scalp and coiled presence of a special-ops veteran. He wore black tactical fabric head to toe but had the easy demeanor of the catcher on your local bar's softball team.

They were in a conference room by his office. He rolled down shades with a remote control device. It was just the two of them.

"Copy that, Commissioner."

"And for the purposes of this meeting, I'm Rick and you're Jeep."

Jeep felt uneasy anyway but showed his best smile.

"Thank you."

"I had your bosses in this morning."

"So I heard."

"And I think *I've* got it tough? Those guys . . ."

He made the universal jerk-off sign, pumping a loose fist. Jeep smiled for real.

"I serve at the pleasure of the mayors," Jeep said.

"And I serve at the pleasure of the county executive, four of 'em and counting, two Republicans and two Democrats. Secret of my longevity?"

"Please. Eight months, I'm still new to civilian bosses."

"Yours do the job for free. Mine gets paid, but makes less than I do. All of them are in it for the power and the glory, but power and glory are reflected states; you need other people believing you're powerful and glorious or it's just two little words. You may not be able to give them what they *want* but you can always give them what they *need*."

"Which is?" Jeep said.

"You pucker up and say, 'of course you're right, of course I will.' Then you do what *you* need to do."

Jeep couldn't know if that's how he actually lasted, but he could certainly sell it by the truckload.

"So I'm *not* going to have County squads combing my streets for car thieves?"

"Of course you are! I promised the mayors!"

His laugh was contagious. Jeep gave in to it.

"Fact is, we're playing Whac-A-Mole same way you are. First cop flips one of them and gets inside the organization, wins. Until then, anything we can do, you just ask."

"Thank you, Rick," Jeep said.

"But next time you catch Ron Arbogast on a DWI? Do me a favor and don't do him any favors."

Jeep's ease disappeared as fast as Knight's smile did.

"How'd you know about that?"

"I'm the Police Commissioner. I know everything."

Jeep couldn't tell if he was half kidding or dead serious. Probably just as he'd intended.

"He *was* a productive cop, a great closer, back in the day. Got a drawer full of medals and commendations. But lately his beat's been between the finer restaurants and the barbershop."

"So get rid of him."

"Guys like him are like barnacles by that age. Pushing retirement, they're fused to the post where the union's concerned. Even guys who got nothing for him don't want to see that precedent happen. Plus his wife's sick, so there's that."

"What's she got?"

"Lou Gehrig's disease."

The pang Jeep got showed on his face and Knight read it.

"There a girl with him?" Knight said. Jeep nodded.

"Asian, in her thirties?"

"Yeah," Jeep said.

"Her name's Mai. But not what it looks like," Knight said.

"How so?"

"You writing a biography of the guy?"

"No."

Knight regarded him for a moment.

"Arbogast's one of those cops collects broken toys. He busted her for prostitution. Bought her sob story, I guess, tried to help her after she did the six months."

"By drunk-driving her around?"

"He got her a gig cocktail-waitressing at an after-hours casino where he moonlights as security. They pull all-nighters together twice a week, make some nice bank."

"And you look the other way."

"Lou Gehrig's, all that home care's gotta cost a pretty penny," Knight said with a shrug. "But looking the other way with him's like a full-time job of its own and I've got twenty-five hundred other cops under my command. Just saying . . ."

"Copy all that," Jeep said.

"The fuck did you say to him?"

"What do you mean?"

"The look you got, like you ran over his puppy."

"Oh," Jeep said, then gave it up. "Something about driving her to the Won't-Tell Motel."

Knight barked a laugh.

"Don't sweat it, I guarantee he's gotten worse."

Jeep's dad used to warn him, "All the good you might do, you can still be judged by your worst day."

Eight Years Earlier

The path to my worst day began when my then-partner Paco and I responded to a domestic disturbance call at a brownstone in Chelsea. The super had called 911 and had a Louisville Slugger in hand in case our response time was as bad as the tabloids had been reporting. He started jabbering backstory but the screaming and the thumping from apartment 2C was all the introduction we needed.

I pounded on the door and announced us as police. The yelling stopped but I did not hear footsteps coming toward the door so I motioned to the super, who had his keys out.

All at once, footsteps on the run, clack of a dead bolt, the door swung open.

She was about thirty and later I'd realize she was beautiful, but in a flash I was past her and grabbing the man halfway out the window to the fire escape. He stumbled back inside and shot his hands up in the air and started huffing about their right to privacy. I asked him if he was carrying a weapon and he said no and laughed like, *do I look like I'm carrying a weapon?* He had shaggy brown hair that fell over his eyes and was all hipster curated like some actor in a magazine you should know who he is but don't. His name was Jasper, we learned. Hers was Laila.

We separated them to the opposite ends of the apartment, which was hers. Paco took Laila and I took Jasper.

He was a freelance photographer, she was an artist who worked part-time as a studio model. They'd been together for six months until a few weeks ago when he'd announced that he had been accepted for a group show on the Lower East Side and he was going to include some of his photographs of her. Which were nudes and some of which, she pointed out, were taken in the hot season of their affair and you couldn't see two of her fingers, if you got her drift. Which made Paco actually gulp and blush.

She had spiky blond hair and high cheekbones that were red and mottled from Jasper's blows. I called for an EMT to check her out.

She said she wanted to press charges, which set him off again, which resulted in his hands cuffed behind his back and an eruption of obscenities as he kicked over a coffee table.

When the EMTs arrived we were free to transport and process Jasper. Laila started to panic; she had a dozen bad scenarios if he made bail, which I admitted was likely. I asked Paco to give her his card and to write his cell number on it, which he did, and when I handed it to her she asked me for mine.

Looking back, I probably should have listened to the look Paco gave me.

I always tried to be a Smart Cop. My dad stressed that Smart Cop makes it to pension and a promising next chapter way more often than Macho Cop, who's more likely to end up dismissed, indicted or deceased. Smart Cop replied to Laila's texts with textbook advice; get an order of protection, call 911 if she feels physically threatened again and inform the 911 operator and the responding officers of the order of protection, the combination of which would likely result in a class A misdemeanor charge and a year in jail if convicted.

Macho Cop, a role my then-partner Paco had down pat, would get the guy's home and work addresses and fuck with him with the impunity of the Shield. If that didn't work, he'd arrange to confront the guy with the irresistible double feature of the Shield and the Gun. Effective, maybe, but a slippery slope for sure.

Smart Cop, however, would have known that while there was nothing in the Patrol Guide specifically forbidding a cop to hook up with a Laila they came into contact with on the Job, it was seen as an unwritten rule and had been since the days she'd have been called a damsel in distress and the Bowery was spelled *bouwerie*.

She decided to get a rescue dog and asked me to help her choose one that could do double duty as pet and protection. I told her I didn't have dogs growing up and had never worked the Canine Unit and really had nothing to offer.

I played with the mutt while she filled out the paperwork and paid the fees. I tried not to bond with him but that's a lost cause with a two-year-old Labrador mix who thinks you're his Lord and savior. She named him Hopper, after her favorite painter.

We walked him all over the Village and talked about how we got there. She was an only child, too, from a town on Martha's Vineyard where the class divisions ran along lines of full-time residents vs. wealthy second-home owners. They had a catchphrase up there, "summer people and summer not," but the tribal signage of club parking stickers and elite college decals was pretty much the same. Her father was a high school history teacher instead of a cop and her merge lane was sailing instead of lacrosse, but the clichés and the customs matched up pretty well.

The walk stopped for lunch, the lunch led to dinner and the dinner turned into the whole weekend. At first I felt like I was in a montage in one of the old Julia Roberts movies my mom loved, but somewhere along the way I stopped walking beside myself and just gave in.

I felt that if I drew a line at the bedroom I could still call myself Smart Cop, but on the third night I crossed the line and by four that morning after I'd come a third time and Laila her fifth or sixth there was no going back and I was *falling in love* in that way people talked about, the sum greater than just the parts of crush and lust.

Jasper started calling her after a couple weeks. She said he was all business at first, calling during working hours, apologetic, and inviting her input on which photographs she would approve for the exhibition. He'd sent proof sheets that she showed me; mostly black-and-white studies of shadows and body parts and a series of her in an old claw-foot bathtub, one with her breasts and labia breaking the plane of the water. She knew what a release was and knew she hadn't signed one; she had a side gig as an artist's model and had posed nude hundreds of times, but always for canvas or sketchbook and none of it licensed for display or distribution with a recognizable depiction of her face.

She shared studio space with some other painters out in Red Hook. One Tuesday she texted me that Jasper was downstairs and arguing with one of the other artists, trying to clear his way up to her. I was out in the field and told her to call the local precinct and mention the order of protection.

Jasper was gone by the time they arrived. He'd gotten into a shoving match with the artist but the guy refused to press charges and instead took it out on Laila, telling her to "clean up her own messes."

Paco offered to "talk to the guy." Which translated as "*you* need to go talk to the guy."

The escalation came slowly at first and then picked up speed. Jasper came around the Red Hook studios twice the next week. Twice Laila called the precinct, twice Jasper fled. But twice was enough for one of the female artists who'd founded the co-op and Laila was asked to pack up and leave.

With Laila's consent I asked the precinct where he lived to arrest him and charge him with violating the restraining order. But he'd moved out of the last address she had for him. His place of business was in Hell's Kitchen, an old-school darkroom lab where he processed and printed his last-century Hasselblad film with their last-century equipment. He owed them for eighteen hours and he hadn't been by in ten days.

The texts and phone calls became a daily then an hourly thing. Laila blocked his number. It helped, until it didn't.

We were in bed, watching TV between bouts. Her phone buzzed, she checked the display and then answered, "Hello." She listened for a second and erupted.

"Jesus Christ, Jasper. You can't keep doing this!"

Apparently, Jasper had gotten himself a burner phone.

I signaled for the phone. She handed it over and burst into tears. His voice was furious static from the speaker. When I spoke up, it was with an even measure of Smart Cop and Macho Cop.

"Jasper, there's a warrant out for your arrest. Get smart. Either turn yourself in or leave town and never try to contact her again."

Friends don't let friends drink and dial. Jasper needed friends. And a straitjacket, the high-pitched craze in his spiel.

"Never mind who this is," I said, and hung up.

It worked. A week went by without a call or attempt at contact, then two. I got the license plates from his car into the plate-readers system but nothing popped in the five boroughs.

Laila still got anxious after dark so I pretty much spent every night there. My own apartment was a white box near the Midtown Tunnel furnished sparsely with a futon couch, a big-screen television and good southern light so there was a fine trade to be made; she moved her paints and canvases in there and made it her studio and I moved some clothes to her place and made it my home.

We spent a weekend on the North Shore that October and stayed one night with my mom, who loved her, and one night with Johnny and Niven, who made a running gag out of poking her or tugging her hair to "see if she was real." As a long liquid night wore on their stories about my near-misses romantic past piled up and had the cumulative effect of anointing me as finally one half of a Great Couple.

Toward the end of the night I helped Niven bus the bottles and glasses to the kitchen. As soon as we were out of earshot she checked the coast and then leaned in close to me and jabbed me in the ribs and whispered, "You fuck this up I'll kill you."

I did, but she didn't.

A few days before Halloween I was walking Hopper on the High Line while Laila made dinner. Only service dogs were allowed on the High Line so I had repurposed some NYPD tags for his collar in case anyone stopped me and I had to peddle some bullshit about how he was an undercover drug-sniffing dog.

My phone buzzed, I answered it.

Laila screamed, "He's in the apart—"

She was cut off. A bang sounded a second later; probably the phone hitting the floor or a wall.

I bolted, yanking Hopper alongside me.

I called 911 on the run, ID'd myself as a cop and gave my shield number, the address, and the situation.

Hopper and I ran a red light across Ninth Avenue, a cab honked and swerved and sideswiped a double-parked panel truck. We kept going.

Her apartment building was in the middle of the block. I still didn't hear a siren. I thanked God I'd taken keys, usually I'd just ring and she'd buzz me up. I also begged Him to spare her.

On the second-floor landing I dropped the leash and reached my off-duty Glock and chambered a round. Hopper followed me to the door to 2C. There was yelling from inside, all him, in that high-pitched crazy tone.

"Fucking cunt queen you fucking cunt!"

I kicked the door open and stepped in.

Jasper had his back against the bookcase with an old-school switch-blade in hand. He was cornered by Laila, who was swinging the fire-place poker in a fierce arc. There was a fire going in the fireplace, one of those wax-and-sawdust bodega logs. Which was a blessing, giving her a quick idea for a weapon.

Hopper barked his head off.

I raised the Glock, aimed right at Jasper.

"Police! Drop the knife and get on the floor!" I shouted.

Laila turned around, her beautiful face twisted in a rictus of fear and loathing.

Two bad moves in one split second; she was smack between me and Jasper, and she'd turned her back on him.

"Get down!" I shouted, but she must have thought I meant Jasper and she just froze. Which gave him enough time to grab her from behind and pull her to him as a shield, the knife at her throat.

Hopper leapt to them and started jumping and barking. Jasper kicked out at him, landing the steel toe of his work boot square in Hopper's muzzle. The dog yelped and backpedaled.

"Jasper, there's nothing we can't walk back here. Let her go!" I said.

"Fucking cunt," he said, moving her sideways toward the window open to the fire escape. "Her Majesty the fucking queen cunt." All in that high-pitched whine.

"Let her go!"

I tried for a bead; he kept moving his head behind hers and I didn't have a clean shot at his legs.

I could hear the whoop-whoop of an RMP coming up the block. About time.

They were in front of the open window. He sat his haunches on the sill and pulled her tighter to him.

He dropped the knife and pulled a plastic squirt bottle from his jacket pocket, like one of those TSA approved-for-travel jobs. He brought it around and crushed it, dousing her face with a stream of clear liquid. All in like, two seconds.

She screamed like she was on fire, which in a way she was. He pushed her off and made to exit through the open window.

I shot once, hitting him in the left eye. He fell back and spasmed a couple times and went still, half-in, half-out.

Laila rolled on the floor, her hands clawing at her face or pushing away Hopper.

I grabbed a dish towel and ran it under the faucet and stooped to her and wrangled it through to her face. She screamed in new pain and shoved at me and then I saw.

Whatever he'd doused her with was making blisters erupt in real time, like a speeded-up nature film. Her right eye was swollen shut and her lips were bubbling blood.

Two cops burst into the room. I reached my shield and held it up.

"Call a bus!" I roared.

They took Laila to the ER at NYU Langone on First Avenue and then right up to the Burn Unit. We'd later find out that Jasper had mixed a cocktail of darkroom chemicals that could eat through matter far stronger than the complexion of a beautiful young woman. That job it handled easily and all too well.

My work-related hell started at the precinct early the next morning, when I surrendered my shield and ID card and was officially placed on modified duty, pending investigation. Next stop was Hudson Street and the Internal Affairs Bureau offices, where I got good-cop-bad-copped by an old pale male and a young Hispanic female.

In my favor, I had called 911 and fully ID'd myself and the potential situation before the face-off and the shooting incident occurred. Also, the fact that it was a one-shot kill by an alert off-duty police officer and not the bam-bam mag dump of a hotheaded boyfriend was a help.

Not so much in my favor was the question of whether the remaining chemical solution in that bottle qualified as a deadly weapon, whether the perp (now vic) was fleeing the scene or posed a clear, present and ongoing danger to Officer Mullane, and last but not least what the fuck was Officer Mullane doing shacked up with a girl he'd met when she'd first called the cops on this piece-of-shit, now-deceased ex-boyfriend.

Her apartment was still a sealed-off crime scene, so Hopper and I were back at mine. He was a good dog but he was definitely *her* dog; in my fresh shock, gnawing misery and growing paranoia I was pretty sure he was giving me a wary side-eye that read *What did you do with her?*

Avoiding Hopper's baleful gaze I looked around my apartment, where almost every eyeline ended on one of her paintings. She'd shown me enough of Edward Hopper's work in books and online that I could recognize the influence or homage or whatever it's called; sun- and shadow-washed landscapes, cityscapes and room-scapes with a slightly out-of-focus aspect and saturated colors.

But in Laila's rendition of a Mobil station on a rural road Eminem was pumping gas, and the nude woman standing in profile in the slash of sunlight from the window was Amy Winehouse. The painting in progress, propped on an easel that looked like a medieval torture device, was of a man in work clothes at a diner counter and the man was clearly me.

I went to the hospital to meet up with her parents, Stephen and Jen. They looked as hollow and strained as I felt. We exchanged some hopeful Googled scenarios but there wasn't a doctor on her "team" who was available for an update and might not be for some time. We traded versions of "so nice to meet you, sorry about the circumstances," and I left them holding hands.

Back at the apartment Hopper had dumped a couple of epic piles of dog shit, one of which I stepped in just inside the door as I reached to hit the lights. I made a bed for him out of an old Hudson blanket and spare pillow and we watched the end of a Rangers game together. I hit the bottle, then I hit the sack and cried.

The next morning I got onto the floor where Laila's room was. I was told in no uncertain terms that she wasn't taking visitors and that visiting hours hadn't started anyway. I waited for Nurse Hatchetface to move along and then I found the room with her name on a card outside and the door slightly ajar. I pushed it a little farther open and looked in.

The blackout shades were drawn and it was dark save for the LED readouts blinking on the equipment displays. With the little light that leaked in I could see she was halfway reclined on the bed, motionless. Her face was wrapped in some kind of high-tech gauze save for slits where her eyes and nostrils and mouth would be. I said her name, quietly. She didn't respond. I said, "It's Jeep," quietly. Still nothing. I left, hoping that she was just sleeping soundly.

The Grand Jury that the Manhattan DA's office convened, as a matter of course, had declined to charge me with any crimes in regard to the incident. The NYPD's Internal Affairs Bureau has different standards for what constitutes a "good shooting" for their officers, and my case was still under review with them.

Johnny and Niven had called and texted constantly. I kept making excuses about letting them take me out in the city or coming out to the North Shore. I'm sure I could have used cheering up but I was also sure I was incapable of it. I was on modified duty as a cop, and as a human being.

Five days after The Night Of I got a text from Laila. She'd checked out of NYU and had landed at her parents' on Martha's Vineyard for a break before reconstructive plastic surgery at Mass General in Boston. She said she was sorry but she couldn't face me with her face right now and added a little sad-face emoji as punctuation. She asked if I could drive Hopper up and that she'd meet me at the ferry at Woods Hole.

Hopper and I were an hour early to meet the 1:30 boat from Oak Bluffs. I got a coffee for me and a bottle of water for him that I poured into the bowl I'd brought. We sat at a picnic table overlooking the water and split a Slim Jim Giant and watched the world go by. Well, he did; I was tense and a little nauseous and couldn't concentrate on a single boat or seagull. I must have reverse-engineered the incident a thousand times by then and still couldn't come up with a better outcome than me as Macho Cop blowing Jasper away while Laila still had him backed against the bookcase.

After what seemed like days of this the ferry from Oak Bluffs was announced over the loudspeakers. I cupped my hand to my mouth and checked my breath. I got the clean bandanna from my pocket and traded it for the filthy one around Hopper's neck, like making him look nice for Mom.

We stood by the rail and watched as the passengers disembarked. I didn't really know what we were looking for exactly; Laila in a mummy wrap, a burqa, a wound-around scarf and Jackie O sunglasses, or miraculously healed. All I knew was that it was my fault and no one could tell me otherwise. I pasted on a smile.

"Jeep! Over here!"

I looked "over here." Laila's mother, Jen, was waving by a pylon near the car ramp. Laila's mother, not Laila.

I tugged the leash and Hopper and I walked over. I kept the smile pasted on, with some effort.

"Laila couldn't make it so she asked me to meet you."

Hopper looked from her to me, like he was as dismayed as I was.

"Couldn't make it 'cause . . ." I said.

She'd met me once, for like, ten minutes. But she had the presence of mind and kindness of heart to let me down as if I'd been in their lives for years.

"Because she's not ready, Jeep. Because she's still in shock, and she's very fragile and still very scared."

"I can imagine," I said. Not only lame, but I actually *couldn't* imagine. So also, bullshit.

"She's so sorry, but there's just no way yet. I could've told her that but she didn't tell me she'd arranged for you to come up until this morning."

"I'm sorry, too."

"How are *you* doing?"

"You know, okay. I miss her." It just came out. She put a hand on my arm.

"I'm sure she misses you too. But her life is going to be . . . quite different for a while as she recovers."

Which was both "so don't hold your breath" and absolutely true, I knew at once. I handed her the leash and squatted down to eye level with the dog.

"Hopper, this is Jen. Jen, Hopper."

She bent down and scratched him behind the ear.

"Hey, Hopper!"

He looked at me like, *What the hell is going on?*

"Jen's taking you to Laila."

At the sound of her name, his ears went up and his tail twitched. I put the icing on the cake, singing to him like I would when I knew she was coming up the stairs or was already at the park, mimicking Erin Clapton's plaintive vocals on "Layla."

Getting barks and a thrashing tail. I kissed Jen on the cheek.

"Thanks for taking the trouble," I said.

"You take good care."

She started for the gangway and I started for the car and I didn't look back.

Two days later I was summoned back down to IAB. They'd reached a decision on my case and it was to be rendered in person. I walked, pushing and pulling in my head whether or not I really wanted to be reinstated. On the one hand, I loved the Job; I went to work every day with a sense of purpose for my life and of belonging to a diverse, dynamic community *in* my life. But given the recent events I was also full of coulda woulda shoulda's and overwhelmed with regret and self-loathing.

Good Cop and Bad Cop wound their way through the formalities and told me I'd been cleared in the shooting. I got a vague feeling that something had been left out.

Which grew when I went before the captain of my precinct. He shook my hand and welcomed me back like we were old partners, though I'd only been in his command for three months. I allowed that maybe it was his routine with good outcomes for his jammed-up cops but I was still waiting for another shoe to drop.

He reached into his desk and got my service weapon and placed it in front of me and then set a Detective's gold shield alongside it.

"Congratulations, Detective Mullane," he said, and held out his hand.

Now it's one thing to be treated fairly in a situation such as mine, which was a by-the-book resolution of a dangerous scenario that by the unwritten code never should have arisen in the first place. It's a whole other thing to be handed the grand prize for it.

I never found out who set the hook and reeled in that shield or whether it was a fight or an easy catch. I grilled my mom and she just gave the usual "That's for me to know and you to find out" she'd pull for *teaching moments* or for when she really didn't know.

My eventual takeaway was that I was a trust-fund kid in my own right. With his service and sacrifice Detective Sergeant Gerald Mullane had left me a fortune in goodwill. It was overseen by trustees who had a sharp eye for what I might need and what I could handle at a given time. The gold wasn't real gold, just an alloy they manufactured the shield with. But I was truly a fortunate son.

I didn't call or text Laila, though it took a lot of effort those first months. Her Instagram page stayed fixed in time since the week before The Night Of.

As a cheat, I took out an online subscription to the *Vineyard Gazette*, the local weekly. I had no idea if she'd actually resettled there, but after a while it became a habit to check it for any mention. A couple of years after there was a notice for her solo show at a gallery in a town called Chilmark, which mentioned an opening reception from five to seven on a Thursday night. I arranged for the time off and bought a round-trip ticket on Jet Blue out of LaGuardia and booked a room at a bed and breakfast.

The morning I was supposed to leave, I walked a couple blocks in her shoes. Her Instagram page had been active for a while by then, with a range of posts: current paintings or cell phone shots of island life or of Hopper on the beach, most drawing compliments or heart emojis in the comments. None of them were selfies.

My cell phone number was still the same one she had in the contacts on her phone, my Gmail account was unchanged, but I'd gotten nothing but radio silence. Being a detective, I could safely deduce that she'd made a choice not to have me in her life again. I could guess at the motives, but guessing was all it would be.

And being a detective, I also knew one thing for certain; showing up uninvited to her gallery opening would brand me as a stalker, plain and simple, to her, and to any cop worth his shield.

So I canceled the flight and the room and wished her well from my safe distance.

Most people think the NYPD's motto is Courtesy, Professionalism, Respect because that's what's lettered on the radio cars. It's not. The motto is Fidelis Ad Mortem. Faithful unto Death.

But she was scarred for life and I didn't suffer so much as a scratch, never mind death. It took me a long time to shake that, if I ever did.

Chapter Sixteen

Jeep's all-day Tour of Shame continued with a return visit to the NCPD's Second Precinct to plaster some gaps in his report from the night before.

There was one consolation prize in store: the Aston Martin DBX stolen from the beach club had turned up abandoned but unharmed on a commercial block in Little Neck, just over the Queens border. Hashing that out with a few of the County's Highway Patrol cops coming off their tours turned into a game of guesses and second-guesses. The odds of a richer target than the Aston sitting pretty on a commercial block in Little Neck were slim and none, so that went away fast. As did the notion of the driver dumping the car because it had been involved in a physical altercation with a police officer and so might bring extra depth and breadth to the manhunt. Jeep eighty-sixed that one himself, observing that the foot soldiers in these operations don't calibrate threat levels; they're just wired to drive from point A to B as efficiently as they can.

But Jeep's own scenario brought them around like Boy Scouts at the campfire. His instinct, harvested from his days as an NYPD detective working with both Gangs and Narcotics, pitched the notion that the car-theft bosses may have their version of a Code Red in place. That would call for all the soldiers in the field to immediately abort mission if one of their number was missing or captured. This would hold until (a) the soldier in question had been released back into the wild and/or contacted his superior or (b) was confirmed as AWOL and was therefore a dead man walking. One of the Highway cops countered with a "c."

"What if we flipped the perp but his bosses don't know it?" he asked. "He could just call in and say he was back out."

Jeep complimented the cop's thinking but set him straight.

"If you're in those crews, they have the addresses of everyone near and dear to you back home. If you flip, they even get a *whiff* you flipped, you're on a hit list you never get off 'til you're dead and they got pictures of your corpse. That's drilled in on Day One, with plenty of visual aids to sear it into your brain."

All of which gave the Highway guys a chill and a thrill. They weren't just chasing knuckleheads in jacked Beemers, they were at war with Bad Guys.

On his way past the Thai Palace a couple blocks west, Jeep tried not to check out the parking lot, tried to miss noticing Detective Arbogast's personal car, tried to convince himself he deserved a break today.

He cut a sharp right into the small lot and parked next to the Cadillac.

Jeep was raised with a mixtape of Copland adages and axioms and Roman Catholic sin-and-penance rosters. Quick and sincere apologies were considered one of the most versatile tools on the belt; they could flavor a confession with genuine regret, set a conflict straight before it could fester into a beef, and soothe the apologist into thinking he was a better person than he actually was. The toughest ones, his mom would say, "bought you a brick for your house in Heaven."

The restaurant was quiet in the early evening. A few senior four-somes shared discounted noodle-and-shrimp dishes at the tables and three solitary patrons were spaced along the L-shaped bar. Arbogast sat at the third-base position, just past the bend. Jeep took the stool next to him. He didn't look over.

"The fuck do you want," Arbogast said.

"I owe you an apology," Jeep said.

"You don't owe me shit," Arbogast said.

Mai, the waitress, was pulling double-duty between waiting tables and tending bar.

"IPA?" she said.

"Club soda, lime. Still in uniform," Jeep said, making a redundant gesture. Arbogast just snorted and rattled his ice.

"And back up the detective here," Jeep said.

Mai got to work. Arbogast had yet to look at Jeep.

"How do you know it's not my fourth or fifth drink?"

"I don't. And it's none of my business."

"But it was last night?"

"Yes, it was. You were driving hammered in my jurisdiction and one of my cops noticed. You set that in motion, not me."

"Then why are you apologizing?"

"You know what? You're being such an asshole, I forgot," Jeep said.

Arbogast laughed and finally looked over at Jeep.

"The balls on you," he said, with a little less vinegar.

Mai set their drinks down. Jeep slid a twenty across. She waved it away.

"On me, for your kindness last night," she said.

"Then in the tip cup," Jeep said.

But she just slid it back across to him, and Jeep respected her by taking it.

"So, sorry for what?" Arbogast said.

Jeep waited until Mai moved off.

"That crack about her and a motel. That crack about your wife putting up with your bullshit. I didn't know the situations."

Arbogast looked away again.

"What, and now you do? How?"

"I had a meeting with Knight this morning," Jeep said.

"About last night?"

"About last night when an Aston Martin got boosted in my confines. Then you came up. He knows about the stop."

"'I'm the PC, I know everything.' He use that on you?"

"Yeah, what is that?" Jeep said.

"He's got a mole in every house is what that is."

Or someone in the chain who's got a beef with you, Jeep thought, but he just let Arbogast be the Man.

"Figures," Jeep said. "Anyway, he clarified your situation for me. I'm sorry for your troubles, and the disrespect I showed was purely out of ignorance."

Arbogast fixed him with a dubious look. Jeep shifted into neutral and just absorbed it. A good apologist knows the importance of body language.

"The fuck you train, Brigham Young University?"

"Just the way I was raised."

"I asked around about you. You had a solid rep in the City. One of the few rose up fast just 'cause of going where the action was."

"As opposed to?"

"Ass-kissing house mouse?"

"I had a hook."

"Yeah, your old man. Everyone knows that. And no one thinks that's why you made detective or why you got the spots you got. In a world where *everyone's* got that shad roe thing."

It took Jeep a moment.

"*Schadenfreude*, you mean?"

"Yeah, that," Arbogast said.

"Well, thanks for the compliment."

"It's not a compliment, it's a lead-in."

"Oh."

"You're practically a kid. Why'd you walk away from the action?" he said.

"I'm thirty-eight. That's only a 'kid' if you're a geezer."

"Why'd you walk away?"

"You know what a chief of police around here makes?"

Arbogast turned on his stool, facing off.

"Why'd you walk away?"

Jeep had a half-dozen stock answers tailored to who was asking, but he'd never been put on the grill about it by an old pro like Arbogast. He tried a new one.

"One, the sheer volume of cases meant too many went cold when they shouldn't have and two, a woman who called us for protection ended up horribly wounded on my very close watch. I tried to shoulder through the caseload, but the memory of the woman, I could never shake the sense that she suffered 'cause of my divided attention."

Neither one said anything. Jeep took a drink of his club soda and wished it was whiskey.

If a good detective leads a person to say things they never meant to admit, Arbogast was good. But if the person under questioning was a detective himself, and knew all the tricks, and was sure he had nailed those boxes shut and buried them ten feet under? If that person told the truth, Arbogast was damn good.

Jeep stood up and put the twenty under the coaster under his glass.

"Didn't mean to go on. Safe home."

Arbogast snorted, shook his head.

"Sorry, couldn't help it," Jeep said. He held out his hand for a shake, and Arbogast took it and closed tight and jerked it toward him, pulling Jeep a little off-balance.

"Easy," Jeep said.

"Look at me."

Arbogast pinned his eyes on Jeep's, like he was looking for his keys in there. Jeep played along for a few moments, frowned and took back his hand.

"What's the matter with you?" Jeep said.

Arbogast just shook his head.

"That favor, your dead friend?" he said.

"Yeah?"

"Her name's Lisa Goldman," he said.

"Whose name is?" Jeep said.

"My ex-partner, now doing PI work for some top-shelf law firms. You'll talk to her."

"How do I find her?"

Arbogast's look like, *try to keep up.*

"She'll find you," he said.

Jeep's phone chimed just as he hit the first red light in the Syosset sequence heading west. The text read: 10pm Long Beach Boardwalk, Westholme Ave betw Lindell and Grand, lose the uniform. LG

Jeep figured the smart money was on the ex-partner doing Arbogast a solid and trying to suss out what, if anything, Jeep had. But being an optimist, Jeep chose to think his act of contrition had moved Arbogast to take a step over to Jeep's side. He calculated fifteen minutes to his office and a change of clothes, forty minutes to Long Beach; he could make it easy, this time of night. He texted back, Copy c u there. A truck behind him long-honked the second the light changed, but he let it go.

There was an expensively potted orchid on his desk and one of those artisanal cheese-crackers-condiments baskets swathed in cellophane and ribbons on the chair in front of the desk.

"Jackson?" Jeep called out.

"Coming, boss!" she replied, from the other end of the trailer.

"Stay outside my door, I'm changing," he called back.

"Here, boss," Jackson said from the other side of the door.

Jeep pulled on his jeans.

"There's like, cheese and flowers in here. Do you know who—"

"They're from the couple, their name is Trip and Alice Stuyvesant they're the folks own the Aston got stolen and then abandoned in Queens and then recovered and now down at Evidence with Nassau PD."

Jeep had on a NY Jets sweatshirt and Nikes by then.

"You can come in now."

Corporal Jackson pushed in, keeping her eyes on the floor.

"Jesus, Jackson, I say 'come in' it means I'm dressed."

"Can't be too careful these days," she said.

Jeep gestured to the booty.

"So, like a thank-you gift?"

"Yes, I mean I think so, you know folks around here they bring a candle or flowers to a dinner party then send a candle or flowers the next day to say thank you," Jackson said.

"We didn't throw a dinner party."

"I think it's just how they're raised. I got a bottle of Dom once from a couple I administered Narcan to their kid at their house."

Jeep rigged his off-duty holster and weapon to his waistband.

"Who'd you tell about the DWI stop?" he said.

"Nobody. Why?"

"'Cause I think there's a mole in our house. Keep an eye on Diaz, will you?"

"Does that mean Diaz's keeping an eye on me?"

Jeep gave her a look of respect.

"You're a smart cop, Jackson. I love that about you. Good talk, gotta go."

Chapter Seventeen

Long Beach on the South Shore of Nassau County is part of the same strand along the Atlantic Ocean as Coopers in Southampton and Two Mile Hollow in East Hampton, and especially on a moonlit Indian summer night you can't tell the difference unless you turn around and face the land. If you're at Coopers or Two Mile Hollow, you see dunes and beach plum and magnificent shingled houses. If you're at Long Beach between Lindell and Grand, you turn right back around and face the water again.

Jeep was leaning on the railing watching a half-dozen surfers, two sitting a set out and the others catching at a break about fifty yards to his left.

A blond woman in a wetsuit and with a shortboard under one arm and an orange knapsack slung over a shoulder came into view, walking up the beach toward him.

She called out, "You Jeep?"

"Lisa?"

She mounted the steps from the beach to the boardwalk and walked right up and shook Jeep's hand. She was of that tribe Jeep called Strong Islanders. From twenty yards she looked to be in her midthirties and then the closer she got the more years came into focus and by the time you shook her hand you realized she was pushing fifty, easy. With each divorce or tragic loss or career setback, the Strong Islander doubled down on herself. She biked, hiked, surfed, kick-boxed, self-helped, hydrated, bleached, waxed and Botoxed her way into a kind of hard-earned beauty that had little to do with genes and everything to do with never giving up or giving in. Jeep loved that tribe and hoped that there would still be some around when he was old and lonely, if only for dinner and a show.

Lisa said, "First off, we never met."

"Second time I heard that today."

"That good or bad?"

"Remains to be seen, I guess."

They moved to a bench and sat a few feet apart. She reached a Kind bar from her knapsack and unwrapped it and bit off half.

She said, "You're going to have questions I could answer but won't, so just listen. I have a client hired me to look into the circumstances of your friend's death. They are aware of you and your peripheral involvement in the investigation."

"'They' as in more than one or could be he or she."

"'They' as in don't talk, just listen."

She reached back into the orange bag and came out with a sealed manila envelope and handed it to Jeep.

"This is the log of his cell phone calls for the month leading up to, and including, Saturday night."

"Courtesy Detective Arbogast."

"Once again, this isn't a Q and A."

"Copy that."

She turned toward him, expression and body language signaling *now this is the important part.*

"There's a third rail here. I have some idea where it is but no real evidence or proof. As Donald Rumsfeld liked to put it, there's 'known unknowns' in play. I do know he or she or they are much higher up the food chain than you are and could certainly cause you to lose your job or worse, you were caught feeling this thing up."

"I won't get caught."

"Said every loser, ever."

Jeep had a thought. In Johnny and Niven's tribe it was customary for one of the parental units, usually the mom, to get the offspring a cell phone when he or she turned eleven or twelve years old. On the North Shore this almost always meant from Verizon, as they had the best cell service in the area. And in that tribe, custody of the account usually stayed with the parents, as it was cheaper and easier to just keep the billing on some Family Plan as the years flew by. So it was not uncommon to be in your late thirties and still have your parents paying your cell phone bill. So there was a decent chance that it wasn't just Nassau PD had access to the dump on Johnny's phone. The account's owner could just punch it up on a website.

Jeep made a leap.

"Please give my best to Gwen," he said.

She was good. She didn't flinch or blink or make a face. She didn't even try a "Gwen who?" She just smiled with dazzlingly white capped teeth.

"Lookit you, trying to trip me up."

She hoisted her stuff and headed back to the ocean.

Driving back north, Jeep made another leap.

He was going down a trail that was, by anecdotal evidence at least, clearly marked with signs reading No Trespassing Under Penalty of You Don't Want to Fucking Know. He had a tough decision to make, as there was also anecdotal evidence that he had a mole in his command, and the Nassau PD hearing that he was on that trail would not be a good look, to say the least.

There were two choices, it seemed to Jeep as he cruised up a mostly empty Meadowbrook Parkway and turned down 1010 WINS to better concentrate. He could follow this down solo, or he could believe that if Corporal Jackson and Sergeant Bondurant weren't loyal, he'd surely know by now. A thought that gave him pause when he considered all the things he thought he knew by now that had turned out, well, *not so much*.

The moment of clarity, once again, came courtesy of his dad. Some wannabe confidential informant, sides for and against his word, but an important case. He told Jeep, "Trust the wrong guy, you're screwed that once. But trust nobody, you're screwed for good."

Jeep called Bondi and told him to round up Jackson and that he'd pick up coffees at a 7-Eleven.

Jackson made copies of the cell phone call logs and each of them took to their desks with their coffees, all three zoned in puzzling out needles in haystacks.

Jeep had a leg up, familiar as he was with Johnny's geography, and he locked in on the area codes of the incoming and outgoing calls in the log for starters. About 95 percent were 212, 516, 631 and 917, which covered landlines and cell phones in Manhattan and Long Island. There were a handful of 561s from South Florida and 310s and 323s from Southern California, all of which would line up with Johnny's orbits.

There were two calls that popped. Both Tuesday afternoon the week of, one incoming and one outgoing, sixteen and twenty-two minutes. Popped because of the extra string of zeros and ones for international calls, digits that came up on Google as being to and from Santiago, Chile.

What Google did not provide was the name of the man or woman who would be answering that mobile number. It was an hour later there. He could call. And if the line picked up and a male voice said *Hola* Jeep could answer *Juan?* and if it was a female voice, he could just say *Catalina?*

A jolt in his head, like synapses colliding, like a thousand watts switched on.

"Jackson!" he yelled out. "That file from Wong, the extract of the burner phone? Get it in here, please?"

Two seconds flat, she was in his office with her laptop open. Bondurant was right behind her, his copy of the logs in hand, alert to the uncharacteristic urgency in the boss's voice.

"Gold in them thar hills?" he said.

"The phone numbers," Jeep said to Jackson. "On the whiteboard, please."

She started copying numbers out on the whiteboard on the wall with a red erasable marker.

Blame it on the hour and the long days and shitty sleep. But Lisbet Woodard's account had finally raised its hand.

"What are we looking for, boss?" Bondurant said.

Jeep pointed at the whiteboard, "One of these burner phones," and poked the call logs, "showing up here the night of."

Jackson wrote down a fifth number on the board: 917-555-5564.

Jeep checked the log like a geezer at a bingo game checking his card.

"Jesus," he said.

"*What*?" they said, at the same time.

"We got a name or a tag with that one?"

Jackson bent to her laptop screen like the closer she got, the quicker the answer might come.

"Angel," she said, after a moment.

"That's the one that vamoosed, right?" Bondurant said.

Jeep said, "Incoming, ten thirteen P.M. Seven seconds, so probably a hang-up. Outgoing, ten fourteen, less than a minute. So maybe, lemme call you back. Outgoing, ten sixteen. Eight minutes. The last phone call he made."

Jeep put his elbows on his desk and his face in his hands.

"Ever," he added.

"Boss?" Jackson said.

For his third and final leap of the night, Jeep went full-on Evel Knievel.

There was a boy named Juan who grew up in Santiago, Chile. He never knew his father, an American tourist who sent money to his mother until he didn't. The boy knew this hurt his mother. The boy grew up on streets where men recruited boys to go to America to steal cars for money. The boy was good at stealing cars, and fearless, and hated Americans for how one of them had abandoned the boy and his mother. The boy learned from his mother that his father once lived, and perhaps still did, on the North Shore of Long Island. Where the boy was stealing expensive cars for money, with other boys from where he was from. The boy would not be able to return with an expensive car for his mother, just some money that would never be enough. But the boy could return with a greater gift: payback. For her broken heart, her hard life, her humiliation. So the boy asked his mother how to contact his father, lying that he just wanted, just once, to meet the man. The boy was an excellent liar, and the mother relented and gave the boy the cell phone number his father had had since he was a boy himself.

"You okay?" Bondurant said.

Jeep looked up at them, neither trying to hide their concern.

"All good," he said. "It's late, let's pick this up in the morning."

He closed the lid of his laptop and stretched as they left the office.

He reopened the laptop and entered JUAN SOTO in the national criminal databases and scrolled through a number of glowering faces and stopped on one.

His look to the camera read as cornered with a side of bemused. His beard was sparse and patchy, like his father's was the one time he tried growing one. His hair and complexion were darker but the geometry of his features was almost identical.

Juan Soto's sheet showed a couple misdemeanor arrests in Miami and noted an aka of *Angel*. Must've been tagged that by his mother, Jeep thought.

When Jeep pulled into his driveway Niven's mother's G-Wagen wasn't there. The whole drive home he'd turned over in his head what he would tell her and what he would withhold, what he thought was possible and what he'd admit was the pure pulp of helpless conjecture.

But if he were being honest with himself, though he was in no mood for that, he'd have to admit that he just wanted her there. To bust his balls, to slide him one of her backhanded compliments, to just be curled up nearby, shooting the shit, all flashing eyes and whooping laughs and just out of reach.

It was no use hating himself for it, Jeep thought. It just was what it was and had been for a long time and he'd get over it, again.

Chapter Eighteen

Jeep had asked Diaz to meet him at the station at seven in the morning and to be wearing dressed-down civvies.

"Check your spam for an email from PhotoCat.com from an hour or so ago," Jeep said.

Diaz was sitting across from him, dressed as ordered, reaching his phone.

"Photomat?"

"Photo*Cat*, with a 'c,' in spam," Jeep said.

Diaz reached his phone, fiddled.

"It says 'warning unknown sender,'" Diaz said.

"I know the sender. Go ahead and open the attachment," Jeep said.

Diaz fiddled some more, frowned.

"What's this? Who's that?" Diaz said.

"This" was a photoshopped picture of Diaz on an urban block with his arm around Juan "Angel" Soto, who was the "that." Detective Wong had taken Soto's mug shot and Diaz's department portrait and worked his magic.

"That's you and your cousin Angel, who you're looking for. Angel Soto," Jeep said.

"Okay. Where?"

"The construction and landscaping crew shape-ups in the parking lots by Home Depot, Long Island Lumber and the Glen Cove 7-Elevens. You're gonna hit them all and show that around and see if anyone's seen him."

"And if they have?"

"Well, take it down. And not in your patrol book, obviously," Jeep said. "You're undercover."

"Even I could figure that. But thank you, boss."

Jeep relaxed a little, without showing Diaz. When he'd hired the kid he knew he was taking a flier with the preening and the cockiness the twenty-six-year-old was still packing from his teenage years. Those qualities can work for or against a cop as he or she settles in to the real life of the Job. You can end up with a charismatic officer who puts citizens at ease and perps on alert, or a loose cannon who goes around believing he's the local "hot" cop and makes more sloppy mistakes than he does good collars. Diaz had come with a strong recommendation from his former CO but Jeep had learned that that kind of enthusiasm can be in service of just trying to get rid of the guy. But he couldn't remember Diaz calling him "boss" before without putting a little spin on it. So, progress.

"Get going. Hit the 7-Elevens first, the landscaping hires usually are on the trucks by eight."

Diaz stood up. "Copy that."

"Oh, and Diaz? You notice there's just the two of us here. We're the only ones in this department know about this op. So if I hear that, say, Nassau PD knows about it too, I'll know it's you who's the mole in my house."

The element of surprise works better the earlier in the day you deploy it. Diaz froze, frowned.

Jeep watched him closely.

"I'm no mole."

"Then who is?" Jeep said.

Diaz faced off with him.

"All respect, boss, I only know who it's *not*. Me."

Diaz looked at Jeep like he was baring his pure heart and clean conscience for Jeep to inspect. Jeep held the look for a long moment.

"That's good to hear, Officer."

Diaz saluted, crisply, and walked out.

Brookside's beach club had an arced jetty that sheltered finger-piers for a couple dozen boats. In the weeks after Labor Day, the club wound down its summer season; the pool was covered, the chairs and chaises stored, and the boats were hauled out, put up on horses, and shrink-wrapped for winter hibernation in the club's parking lot.

The boathouse manager, Gus, was making his final rounds of inspection before heading to Delray Beach for his other seasonal gig when he noticed a hole had been torn in the wrapping on a Grady-White Tournament 25. He thought it was raccoons as usual until he widened the opening with his pocketknife and called the police. While raccoons would certainly enjoy the KFC and Entenmann's Crumb Cake from the buckets and boxes strewn around, they couldn't have uncapped all those bottles of Modelo.

Bondurant bagged an empty bottle for possible prints as Jeep took an inventory.

Bondurant said, "Wish he'd made a campfire, we could figure the time since that varmint vamoosed."

Jeep wondered if Bondi kept a brass spittoon under his desk. He'd remember to check.

Jeep held up a Rite Aid receipt he'd reached from a plastic bag.

"He was here yesterday, at least," he said.

A shopping trip had brought a three-pack of men's briefs, Extra

Strength Tylenol, a box of energy bars, a bumper crop of Slim Jims
and Pringles, and a couple gallon plastic jugs of Poland Spring water.
The boat's cushions had been repurposed into a bed and pillows in the
stern belowdecks and the toilet in the head was ripe.

Jeep's mind kept racing around the same circular track, where the
banner over the starting line read, "If It's Him": Why stick around?
You're a car thief, why not help yourself to a damn car? Did you
go on the errands yourself, or did some confederate bring you the
supplies? And who the hell offs his own father, if that's what happened, and then sets up camp nearby? The only thing he thought
he knew for certain was that if you were fleeing the scene from The
Night Of, stowing away on a boat in this lot was the nearest sheltered
hideout.

Mayor Donahue interrupted Jeep's reverie with "Now we got a mi-
grant camp?! What the fuck!"

Jeep scrambled down off the boat and steeled himself as Donahue
rolled up.

"We don't know who it is."

"Who else lives in a dry-docked boat?" Donahue swerved around
Jeep and hoisted himself up for a look.

"What's that smell? Jesus!"

"Please step away, Mayor, we're still going through it."

"Remember that kid, the Boston Marathon bomber? They found
him in a stored boat!"

"Sir, this isn't that," Jeep said.

"Oh, oh! Right you are! No bomb went off—yet!"

"Mr. Mayor, what are you doing here?" Jeep asked as politely as he
could manage.

"I got a call from Chase Hubbard, Brookside's president. Do you
have any idea how humiliating that is?"

"I can only imagine—"

"No, you can't! I had two Job Ones when I was elected—get a

Police Department up and running and get a cell phone tower built so we could reliably nine-one-one that goddamn police department! And where'm I at? Bunch of woke tree-fuckers blocking my tower and Barney Fife for a sheriff?!"

Bondurant, uncharacteristically, stepped in.

"Actually, the old *Andy Griffith Show* had Sheriff Andy and *Deputy* Barney Fife," he said.

Donahue leveled a glare at him, Bondurant stood his ground, and Jeep briefly revisited that '60s television fantasy of his job: a small-town sheriff solving mild crimes with corny schemes and folksy wisdom.

"And now illegal encampments? Tell me, Mullane, is there no end in sight to this shitshow?"

"Yes sir, there sure is," Jeep said as he turned to Gus. "Is there surveillance on this lot?"

"Supposed to be. I'll check it's working."

"Sergeant Bondurant will assist you and we will need the footage if the cameras are in fact working."

"Of course," Gus said.

"Bondi, I'll put Ellis and Rigby out canvassing and have Jackson come down and assist in ID'ing and securing the rest of the evidence in the boat here after you review the footage."

"Copy that, boss."

Donahue had slunk away, quickly bored when the focus moved off him, as Jeep had hoped.

Jeep's ruse was a framed color photograph clipped out of a *Newsday* Sunday sports section from twenty-one years ago. It was in an inexpensive Lucite frame, one of many his mom used to have on hand for just that kind of thing; to respect a moment in time that might otherwise end up in the kitchen dead-batteries drawer. If you framed it, even in cheap plastic, and stood it on a bookshelf or dresser, then it wasn't fleeting at all but a daily drive-by past that fine day. The photograph was an action shot of Jeep and Johnny in a leaping high five, with a desolate goalie sprawled on the turf behind them.

It was a ruse in that if Pete Chambliss was home, Jeep could just say he was dropping it off as another keepsake of Johnny's vibrant youth. If Pete was not at home, Jeep could use it as a prop to help pry Gwen open.

He found her out back, by the roses bordering the patio. She'd added a Patagonia fleece to her gardening getup, as the morning had brought the first real chill of autumn. She was cutting the roses instead of tending them, putting the long stems in a basket.

"Good morning, Gwen." It was the first time in history he'd called her by her first name without being commanded.

She looked over, shielding her eyes against the low sun.

"Hey you!"

He walked over to her, holding the frame at his side with the photograph turned in.

"Sorry to just show up like this."

"You're always welcome here," she said.

"Do you have a couple minutes?"

"Do *I*? I think that's more a question for our busy Chief of Police!"

She smiled at him. The lines around her eyes and mouth seemed more pronounced and the light in those eyes seemed dimmed. But that was to be expected, he thought.

She blinked back tears and set the frame on the coffee table in front of her, facing away.

"Oh, my. I just never know what'll turn on the waterworks these days."

She smiled and waved a hand in front of her face, as if shooing away a gnat.

"I'm sorry. I should have waited," Jeep said.

"No, no. Any memories like that one, I say *bring 'em on*."

She could brighten again in an instant, like there was a light switch she could find in the pitch dark.

"So thank you, Jeep," she said, using his nickname for the first time in history.

"He was a great guy," Jeep said.

"I think so, too."

"Who some people judged solely by his worst days and bad choices. People who should know better, or at least take a look in the mirror before they, you know, throw that stone."

Gwen just looked at him with her warm smile frozen in place.

"Are you here as a cop?"

"As a cop, as an old family friend, but mostly as a man who likes to know what's really what. *Needs* to know."

"And why do you *need* to know?"

"Same reason you do, maybe. Same way we'd want to know, say he died in a single-car accident, (a) was he blind drunk, (b) did a tire blow out or (c) did someone run him off the road."

She weighed it, looking away.

"I thought he died in a boating accident."

"I don't think that's the whole truth," Jeep said.

"I don't think we *can* know the whole truth, about much of anything."

"You know he had a son, right?"

She just nodded, yes.

"Your grandson's been in the area. Your grandson called Johnny last Saturday night."

"Stop calling him that."

"Why?"

"Because you're saying it like it's some kind of dig. Have some respect and kindness or please leave."

She pinned him with a look he'd never seen but could imagine who had; Pete's mistresses and Pete himself, when she confronted him about those mistresses. Johnny's fake-concerned heads-of-school with their fake-pained expressions. Niven, over God knows what she'd been told to say or do or not say or do as a newly minted Chambliss.

"And what are you saying?"

"You're going to have to be more specific, Mrs. Chambliss."

She smiled, rising to the challenge like a champ.

"Well, Chief Mullane, we were talking about my son's passing and you tossed a grenade."

"I'll assume you know your husband had the boy and his mother cut off, years ago," Jeep said.

"I thought that was a mistake and said so at the time."

"But it was done anyway. What you may not know is that the syndicate of car thieves working this area was born in Santiago, Chile, as was the boy."

She flinched and shook her head.

"Where are you going with this?"

"Around and around. I could use some directions."

She stood up abruptly and went to the French doors and opened one a crack and then another, then another, then back to the first, readjusting the size of the opening.

"Ask me a question," she said.

"Did your husband ask the police to sit on anything about last Saturday night?"

"Could you be a little more vague?"

"Did your husband ask the police to ignore the scratches on your son's back and pressure the ME to sign off on 'accidental' as the cause of death?"

"I thought *you* were the police. Why ask me?"

"The Nassau PD. The ones charged with investigating."

"What's an ME?"

"The medical examiner."

"Then why not just say that?"

"Screw this," Jeep said to himself, but just loud enough for her to be copied on it. He stood.

"Sorry to take up your time, Mrs. Chambliss."

She shot back at him, sharp and loud.

"Well, look who's afraid of a little hard work! Now sit the fuck down and call me Gwen from now on, got that?"

Jeep swallowed it and sat down. Gwen Chambliss shouting "fuck" at him was like she'd willfully ripped a loud fart, shocking and unsettling.

She went to the sideboard bar and chose a bottle of something brown and the cork squeaked as she uncapped it.

"Would you like a drink?"

"Little early for me," he said.

"For me, too."

She poured some into a crystal tumbler and sat down on the couch right next to him in a way that seemed both aggressive and comfortably familiar, at once. She took a swallow and put the glass on the coffee table on top of a large-format book titled *Long Island Country Houses and Their Architects*. She leaned back and crossed her arms and stared straight ahead.

"There's a lot my husband doesn't discuss with me, there always has been. But leaning on the police? No. Pete always likes to cut out the middleman, and cops are middlemen, no offense."

"None taken. Who would he go to?"

"The county executive, Trace Barnett. He and Pete have gotten close over the years. Partly the business of bundling money for him, but also long weekends bonefishing in the Bahamas, just the two of them and the guides."

Bonefishing was another rich-person pursuit Jeep couldn't fathom; long journeys to torrid flats trying to catch an elusive fish that no one ever ate.

Gwen continued, "Not that I know they cooked anything up."

"So, a lot you *don't* know. What's something you *do*?"

She frowned, clearly annoyed.

"Okay, two things. One, Pete and his friends have statewide and even national plans for Trace. Which means you're never going to get 'the goods' on him in this matter or any other because, two, and this is the important part, Pete hates messy. Pete *fears* messy. Thinks messy is weak and practically immoral, and if he so much as gets a glimmer that someone is messy, Pete cuts them off. But you know that."

She reached out for her glass and took another drink and passed it to Jeep like to gently remind him that good manners dictate a gentleman doesn't let a lady drink alone. Jeep drained the glass.

"Pete hasn't been Pete for this long by forgetting to lock up the safe," she said.

"But it's your son, *his* son. You must've talked about it, shared your doubts."

"And he hasn't been Pete for this long by entertaining doubts."

"But you do have yours," Jeep said.

She hit pause, reaching the glass and tipping the last drop to her lips.

"Why else hire Lisa Goldman?" he added.

She wasn't that good an actor. She held a breath, let it out, practiced and measured, like some relaxation technique she'd learned in some class, as Jeep's pet theory flew out the window. Gwen hadn't authorized Arbogast; he had acted on his own, or for somebody not Gwen.

"I don't know what you're talking about," she said.

"Have it your way."

She looked at him, clearly lost.

"How do you know about her?"

"I'm the Chief of Police. I know everything."

The Nassau PC pulled it off way better. Jeep's fallback was just to return Gwen's frown with a shrug.

"I don't know if or how the boy is involved. But if you find him, I wish to meet him. He's all I have left of my Johnny."

"Careful what you wish for," Jeep said, after a moment.

"I didn't wish for any of this. And I'm sick and tired of being careful."

She slumped, spent.

"Johnny once said you had the hardest job of any mother he could think of because you also had a full-time job serving as his father's ambassador to his children. He loved you for that, too."

She started to cry. Jeep thought of what a gentleman would do and decided it would be to gently put an arm around her.

She leaned into him and rested her head on his shoulder.

Six Years Earlier

I was driving south on the FDR, on my way back to the squad after getting pulled off a stakeout in East Harlem when the quarry was collared at a Jersey Mike's in the Newark Airport. My cell phone buzzed, the display read NIVEN, I picked up.

"Hey."

"I need you to come to their apartment right *now*—"

"Wait, *whose*?"

"Pete and Gwen's, Eight Sixty-Six Park—"

"I know where it is."

She responded to something I couldn't hear, yelling her reply.

"I'm on the phone with Jeep!"

More urgency in reply; I couldn't make out the words.

"I think he's in the kitchen but I'll go look. You stay where you are!"

She came back to me.

"It's really fucked up here, please hurry."

The line went dead. I hit the lights and sirens and cut across two lanes and just made the Ninety-Sixth Street exit.

. . .

Eight Sixty-Six Park Avenue was an Emery Roth–designed apartment building that was built in the early 1930s and had a well-earned reputation for being ominously selective in regard to who was allowed to buy in and live there. To the residents of 866, rich techies were seen as technocrats bent on world domination, stars of screen and stage as carnival geeks and amoral pagans, and the mustachioed Monopoly moneybags guy was wholly aspirational. Even the doormen and porters were thoroughly screened to confirm they were from the "desirable" enclaves in Lithuania and Slovakia. One of them, Jozef, politely stopped me at the door.

"May I help you, sir?" he said.

I opened my coat to show him the shield hanging on the chain around my neck. I have always favored the hanging chain over the belt clip or flip wallet; it styled like an all-access backstage pass to the Depraved Indifference tour.

"Going to Chambliss, Penthouse A. *Quietly.*"

"Of course, sir. I'll just ring up."

"You ring up, I'll be in the elevator."

Niven took me to Pete first, navigating the hallways with her one good eye as she held a bag of frozen corn niblets over the other. I'd noticed the pancaked coffee table and broken glass in the library on my way by.

"Have you called nine-one-one?"

"No, I called you," she said.

Pete was laid out on his back on the bed in the master with bath towels all around him to soak up the blood running from lacerations on his forehead and, I learned when I gently lifted off the washcloth he held to it, a broken nose.

"What hospital?" I said.

"What do you mean, what hosp—"

"Where you give money, where your doctor has privileges."

"Oh. Carnegie Hill-Nightingale."

Where there would be a private suite available to him, one of a discreet collection where elite donors are tended to as if they'd checked into a Ritz-Carlton and not an inner-city ER.

"Sit tight," I said.

Johnny was at the kitchen table with a lower lip burst like an overripe tomato and hunched over holding his side. His heavy breathing had a little whistle to it.

"What hurts?" I said.

"Think he broke a rib."

He winced with each word.

"Maybe punctured a lung, way I'm breathing."

"Find a place to stretch out, I doubt that position's helping any."

I jerked my head at Niven, who helped him to his feet, and they walked off like a doddering elderly couple.

"And reach Pete's doc, tell him we're headed to the ER at his hospital," I called after them.

I dialed the one-nine precinct and got hold of the captain, Clifton, who came up under my dad. I requested an ambulance at the service entrance to 866 Park going straight to the ER at Carnegie Hill-Nightingale. I asked him not to ask questions but he did anyway. I was straight with him but also told him I might be fudging some when we got to the hospital. He signed off with a "good luck."

As we rode down the elevator I briefed all three of them on my fresh new version of what exactly had happened before I got there, who the assailant was, and told them to let me do the talking when we got to the hospital. No one objected.

Which turned out not to be necessary as all three were whisked away on gurneys moments after we pulled up. I was left with the hospital's police liaison officer. She was in her forties and wore low "fun" sneakers in New York Mets colors and had a form on a clipboard and a pen in hand.

"What happened here?" she said.

"There was an intervention that went bad, apparently."

"Apparently?"

"Yes. By the time I got there the assailant had fled."

"Do you know the name of the assailant?" she said.

"Glen Rove. He's an old friend of the family who's developed a serious drug problem that the vics were confronting him about. You've heard of Flakka?"

Flakka, aka Gravel, was a street synthetic that acted like morphine until a component kicked in that turned the user into the Incredible Hulk. An enthusiast in Atlanta had flipped a Honda Civic on its side, just for kicks and all by himself.

She frowned. "Of course I have."

"That's his drug of choice. He was high on it when they attempted the intervention, which they didn't know. He went off."

"You got all this at the scene?"

"I'm an old friend of the family myself."

"Who just happened to catch the nine-one-one dispatch?"

"No, they reached out to me directly."

"Family has a lot of friends, do they?"

"Yes, they do. Including many right here at this hospital."

"What's the name again?"

"Chambliss," I said.

"As in, the Chambliss Oncology Pavilion?"

"That'd be them."

I gave her a look like inviting her to join Team Compassion.

"What a world," she said with a sigh.

"Tell me about it," I agreed. "Now, I got to go finish my reports, if that's okay with you."

The shield bought me two minutes with Johnny, who was in a screened-off hospital bed and hooked up to an arsenal of sucking and beeping machinery. An IV dripped a sedative into his veins. It made him a little loopy, doing its job.

"Find out what brand this is, it's fantastic," he said.

"Yeah, okay. What happened?"

"I asked him to help me help Haiti. He'd provide two mil in funding and I'd provide boots on the ground, including myself. All that fucking French finally coming in useful."

Haiti had just been in the news having taken yet another one-two punch of natural disaster and explosive civil unrest.

"Well that sounds like a non-starter, even I could've told you—"

"Every journey begins with a single step."

I couldn't tell if that was the drugs talking or something he'd picked up along the way and bent to the matter at hand.

"Okay, and this big ask started . . . what?"

"We both said some shitty things, then he said a *really* shitty thing and tried to push me out of the library, like, physically. I pushed back, he threw the first punch."

Pete Chambliss had been the champion of his college boxing club and was still fierce in the ring all those years later at the New York Athletic Club and apparently in his library at 866 Park as well.

"Being honest with myself? If I can't do for others, I'm nothing. I'm a sack of shit in a blazer and khakis."

The sedative unlocked the same sudden-onset self-loathing that extra drinks could; I'd seen it many times before and had tried many ways to move him off it.

"But a fine calfskin, silk-lined sack of shit," I said.

"Don't laugh at me," he said.

"I'm not."

"Yeah, you are. It's fucking condescending, like you think I'm looking for sympathy. I'm not."

"All right, easy, man . . ."

"You know I paid your college tuition? Did you know that?"

And there it was, coming up in a way I never saw coming. I had a split second to answer with an honestly surprised expression on my face.

"No, I did not."

I'd been a cop for a while by then and was pretty good at closing the sale on a lie.

"You know why? 'Cause even as just a kid I knew my friendship alone was like, I don't know, a semi-decent party; okay for a while but easy to split the moment the beer ran out. I'd need something concrete to make anything last."

"For that to be true, I would've had to know you paid back in the day, no? I'm just here 'cause I thought we *were* friends all this time."

"But you knew. Your dad or mom must've told you."

"Didn't happen."

"Dude, I can tell when you're lying, always could and you know it."

"Nope," I said.

"Yup," he imitated me. "Why didn't you ever bring it up? To thank me, or get all pissedoff at me? And please look at me when I'm talking to you."

I did. And then I said, "Okay, thank you and fuck you."

"You're welcome and fuck you, too!"

I laughed, surprising myself. He laughed but it clearly stabbed him hard, how he winced.

I'd come to regret that we didn't take the moment to do a deeper dive, but that's how we'd always rolled; splashing each other in the shallow end, respecting the code of suburban teenage jocks even as we passed thirty.

And Johnny's self-drawn portrait was a lot like the one my dad described him peddling when he offered to gift my tuition; of a guy convinced that all he really had to offer was cash or connections. So maybe it wasn't the drink or drugs talking when he'd turn on himself, maybe it was that in vino veritas thing, what he really did see in the mirror.

But the screen zipped open behind me and a doctor and two nurses came in and the nurses descended on Johnny and the doc ushered me out.

Niven was in the waiting room with a hospital-issue KoldPak on her eye that probably cost her insurance five hundred dollars and change. I sat down next to her.

"Johnny'll be here tonight at least. What about Pete?"

"A car's taking him back to Long Island. The only plastic surgeon he trusts is in Huntington."

I leaned in for a closer look. She turned away.

"How's the eye?"

"Cold," she said.

The waiting room was sparsely populated; a few walking wounded fidgeted in their seats and fiddled with makeshift bandages while their buddies or next of kin played with their cell phones.

"Haiti? Seriously? The hell'd *that* come from?" I said.

"Very serious. It's like, all he talks about. Some techie Georgetown friend is all in with Sean Penn, who's the, like, celeb spokesman for helping Haiti. Johnny had dinner with him in L.A. last month."

"Dinner with Jeff Spicoli. *Awesome*," I said.

"And promised to raise money but had to get Pete on board. Instead, Pete gave a lecture on the tragic history of Haiti and good money after bad. Then the fun started."

She shook her head and groaned.

"This is one of those nights I wish I still smoked." She removed the KoldPak and turned to me.

"How bad?" she said. The socket was turning purple and her eye was swollen shut.

"Who hit you?"

"Nobody. I caught an elbow trying to break them up. How bad?"

"Tied with the Chicken Fight at Lacey Berrien's pool party."

In eighth grade, where Niven had tried to pull off her opponent's bikini top on a dare and caught a fist for it.

"Ugh," she said.

"Drop you somewhere?"

"I'm going to check with the docs then go clean up the apartment some. But thanks."

I patted her knee and stood up.

"Wait a minute?"

Something in her tone; I sat right back down.

"I guess Johnny didn't tell you or you'd have brought it up. We're getting a divorce."

"News to me," I said, and it was.

You see signs, sure. You ask, "Everything okay with you two?" You get a "Marriage can be hard" and a "But I'm not going anywhere" that has a sad, surrendered edge to it. And if you're chronically single like I was, you just don't have the on-the-job experience to add up all the little telltale clues.

"The final straw was him committing to a year on the ground in Haiti, funding or no funding, with me or without me."

"The final straw, okay," I said. "But the main reason?"

"He doesn't want kids."

"He said that?"

"In so many ways."

"You don't think he'll come around?"

"The longer we put it off, the lamer and weirder the excuses get. I mean, come on, a year in Haiti, who does that? Kids were always part of our deal. Or so I thought, anyway. But the more time goes by, the more he gets like his father, all 'trust me on this, it's for the best.'"

Which was another aspect I'd clearly missed. When a man spends as much time over as many years as Johnny had in framing his father as a cautionary tale, you feel bad for the son, but you don't think to put him side by side in a lineup with the father. Or at least, I didn't. I began to realize that what skills I had as a detective on the streets weren't carrying over to my private life.

"And I don't want to end up like Gwen Chambliss. Well, except for her tennis game and her still-perky tits," she said.

I laughed, as was my duty.

She tossed the KoldPak in the wastebasket nearby.

"Take me out of here, please."

"You don't want to talk to the doc?"

"No. I don't want to pick up after their mess, either. I want to go have three drinks and an order of fries and be put in a cab. My work here is done."

Johnny did go to Haiti, without one thin dime from the family pot. He spent eleven months there fitting in as a kind of utility logistics guy specializing in temporary housing, putting local talent together with United States, United Nations and various privately funded relief organizations. The cell phone photos he sent charted a rake's progress from earnest do-gooder tacking up blue tarp roofing on dilapidated shacks to a long-haired, deeply tanned Jack of All Trades posing with ever-growing groups of locals, armed with a bottle of rum and a winning all-American grin.

As it turned out, Johnny didn't need deep pockets to make connections; his chronic insecurity and need for approval combined with old-school manners and self-deprecating charm translated well enough, plus eight years of French didn't hurt. Just in case, I gave him the cell phone numbers of a series of NYPD Emergency Service Unit cops posted down there; he only reached out to one, and that was to help him out of a jam not of Johnny's own making.

He returned, under a deal with Niven, to seek marriage counseling together in a last-ditch effort to at least respect their vows and honor their shared past. She'd told me, though I doubt told him, that she hoped he'd fall hard for some poor abandoned newborn and they could cobble together a future based on "nobody getting everything they wanted, just enough of what they needed."

But Johnny landed at JFK with empty arms, and the divorce became final just after Christmas that year.

Chapter Nineteen

Officer Diaz had parked his Solar Orange Subaru WRX out of sight in back of the trailers and was pulling the custom-fit cover over it, still buzzed from the chase.

"I noticed they kept changing lanes on Cedar Swamp like to keep on my tail. Then they pulled up alongside when I took the left onto 25A and I figured they were looking to race. They were in a GTI, and GTI versus WRX is like, classic."

Jeep tugged the cover off the hot tailpipe, his "fire hazards" OCD making a surprise appearance.

"Anyway, this *escoria* riding shotgun shows a Glock and waves it like for me to pull over and I'm like, fuck that. I hit it hard and they ride my bumper 'til the light by the tech college and I drift the left onto Valentine's and lose 'em."

Jeep hadn't meant to make Diaz into bait with the assignment, but that seemed to be the upshot. Showing Angel's picture around at the strip-mall shape-ups got some kind of telegraph system up and running and by the time Diaz left the Glen Cove 7-Eleven the word was out, along with the make, model and plate number of his personal car. Should've thought of that, Jeep thought.

"You get their plates?" Jeep said.

"Yeah, Bondi's in there following up."

Not that what popped would win any chicken dinners, Jeep thought. Either the plates were stolen or the whole car was.

"Boss, one thing, and please tell me if I'm out of line, I'll accept that. But it's my *ride*, you know? And now it's got these two dirtbags got the make, model and plates looking for it. I mean, I'm out on a date and all of a sudden, what, she's looking at a Glock pointed . . ."

He broke off, tugged the cover tight over a headlight.

"We'll get you a temporary ride. And good work out there, Officer."

Which was more than Jeep could say for the Chief of Police who sent him.

Bondi had entered the bad guys' GTI's tags into the villages and county plate-reader database and was able to track it east on Northern Boulevard until it had turned onto Redcoats Road just past Oyster Bay Cove. Redcoats was a residential dead end and so normally wouldn't have a plate reader but besides a dozen or so modest houses it was home to the Briarcliff School, a private day school founded in the sixties in a repurposed old estate. There had been an incident the previous year where a second-grader was snatched from the Free to Be Me Wellness Center, which was what the donor family had named the refreshed playground. The boy was quickly located with his father, a Forge Foresight partner involved in a nasty custody battle who had violated an order of protection in taking young Harrison to a Mets game. But an armada of helicopter parents were so alarmed they paid up to wire the whole place for video surveillance, hire three full-time security guards, and raised thirty-nine thousand dollars to install a license plate reader outside the school's entrance pillars on Redcoats Road.

Jeep rolled by the split ranches and phony Colonials, looking for the GTI and striking out. But at the end of the road an older house had been razed and the foundation for a new one poured. A half dozen workmen to-and-fro'ed with loads of wood and wheelbarrows of mixed concrete. Coach's Dodge Ram was parked by the porta-potty.

Jeep headed back up the road, pulled over, and texted the cell number he still had from his playing days.

"Yeah, one of those hot hatches they like so much. Pulled up around nine thirty, one of the guys on my crew, Julio, went over to it, started talking to the two guys in it 'til I yelled at him to get back to work."

Coach had met Jeep by the boat launch in Oyster Bay. They were parked side by side with the windows down.

"Talked to them? Laughed with them, argued with them?"

"It was quick, I couldn't say." Coach shook a Marlboro Red from a box on the dash and lit up. "Julio's good people, five years on my crew. He in some kind of trouble?"

"Not that I know of."

"Listen, I'm sorry about the other day. And thank you for . . ." He broke off, taking a deep drag. "I haven't had a drink since."

"I guess that's good."

"So far, so good. I don't know what got into me."

"Everyone's looking for someone to blame for their shit," Jeep said.

"But spitting on a guy's casket? That ain't me. Least, it didn't used to be."

He suddenly flicked the cigarette out the window, like he'd had a flash maybe smoking was part of his problems, too.

"You ever hear this Julio or the others talking about a guy named Angel?" Jeep said.

"Yeah, I have. Who's he to you?"

"A person of interest, as we say in the biz."

"They were talking about him again after the hot hatch left. About how the hot-hatch guys had heard Angel was still around. I'm pretty good with Spanish by now."

"Talking like there was a reward or something, some prize for who fingered him?"

"Nah. The way Julio was talking to Mateo, more like it was bad news for Angel that these guys knew he was still around."

"Mateo and Julio, where are they from?" Jeep said.

"South America, I think from Chile?"

Jeep kept his cool.

"You got addresses?"

"I can get. And it'd be the same address. These guys, I get the feeling it's like ten to a bed."

"Be a huge help."

"You sure Julio's not in any trouble? I can't lose him."

"He's not in any trouble with me, that's all I can guarantee. Never heard of him before just now."

Coach looked at Jeep for a long moment, like he was trying to remember what trust felt like.

"I'll find the paperwork and text it."

"Can't thank you enough, Coach. And this stays just between us."

"Works for me. And it's been a while since I was any kind of coach, Chief."

"It's how I know you," Jeep said.

Jeep's intel was decent enough to give it a try, especially since he'd had unrelated business at the NCPD's Second Precinct just three minutes away.

He found Arbogast's Caddy in the lot parked way in the far corner; a longer walk from any of the shops but safe from door-dings from idiots, which Jeep respected. He pulled in backward so he could face Anthony's A Cut Above Salon and waited. After five minutes, Arbogast came out, checked his reflection and fixed his tie in the Woodbury Wine Shoppe display window, and came striding toward his car. When he was about ten yards out, Jeep showed himself.

"The fuck?" Arbogast said.

"Gimme sixty seconds," Jeep said.

"You're starting to remind me of Long Covid, you know that? Just when I thought I was done . . ."

"You're wasting my sixty seconds."

"I didn't *grant* you sixty seconds."

He chirped the locks open with the fob and blew past the Tahoe. His cheeks were red from a hot shave and his hair was perfect.

Jeep said, "It wasn't the PC told you to look the other way."

Arbogast looked around like to see if anyone could be within earshot, then at Jeep, incredulous.

"Nobody told me to look nowhere."

"Almost."

"The fuck's that mean?"

"The county executive told you to look *nowhere*."

"You want me to step over there and beat the shit out of you?"

"No," Jeep said. "Just tell me I'm wrong."

"Some fucking nerve."

"Sixty seconds is up."

Jeep moved fast, back into the Tahoe and pulling out in like, two seconds. It worked.

Arbogast was running alongside and slapping at the driver's side window.

"STOP THE FUCKING CAR," he shouted.

Jeep jumped on the brakes and powered down the window. Arbogast's head filled the space, wafting bay rum, volcanic.

"You listen to me. Rick Knight's clean, know that. You just keep your eyes on the prize and forget about everything else. You think your dad wants you to be a great cop, or a great *whistleblower*? And no, you can't be both."

He was panting, his eyes watering.

"Cop," Jeep said.

"Then do right by him, right by your friend, leave the politics to the old hairbags."

He reached in and scuffed Jeep's head, like some tough-love Big Daddy move. He pushed off and walked back to his Cadillac and Jeep accelerated out of the lot with a full heart and a dizzy brain.

Jeep had done a drive-by on the Glen Cove address Coach had texted him. It was a faded-green vinyl-sided job with fake-brick accents, the saddest-ass house on a block of close runners-up. There was a beater Nissan Maxima with fat aftermarket pipes and a rust-bucket nineties Ford F-150 parked out front. A chain-link enclosure in the side yard penned a couple of sleeping pit bulls and had three bicycles fastened to the stanchions with U-bar locks that were likely more valuable than the bikes they secured.

"Why don't you just knock on the door and question this Julio and the other guy," Jackson said. "The worst that can happen is they just clam up, right?"

Bondi, Jackson and Diaz were crowded into Jeep's office with the door closed.

"No, no middlemen," Jeep said. "Or warrants, or subpoenas. Remember, this isn't our investigation. And we don't know that this Julio and his pal don't already have eyes on them."

"Like whose?" Diaz said.

"The ring's bosses. The ring's bosses' muscle, those guys followed you this morning. We don't know what side Julio's on, if he's even on one."

Bondurant's knees were jiggling up and down, like he was agitated by what was banging around in his head and anxious for a turn.

"Bondi?" Jeep said.

"Why aren't we just handing this off to Nassau PD? I mean, they are the capital 'L' law this side of the Queens line."

Jeep shifted into neutral, taking a look around. Clearly Bondi had said what was on other minds as well.

"That's a good question, and I wish I had a good answer. But all I've got is my gut, and my gut is this: In the NYPD they had a term for when a bad guy killed a worse guy. They called it an 'act of community service,' like, everyone was better off for it, no harm no foul. We know Johnny Chambliss talked to this Angel the night of, which means they very likely do too. But so far as I can tell, they haven't made a single move on it. Which makes me think powers that be gave Nassau orders to stand down and wait until somebody steps up and performs a community service and puts this to bed for good. And one other thing, never to leave this room?"

All eyes on Jeep. He told the truth and nothing but, with some difficulty.

"Johnny was my friend and I want to honor him by finding out what happened in the minutes before he died last Saturday night. What happened between him and this Angel, last Saturday night. Who said what, who did what. 'Cause see, Angel's given name is Juan, Spanish for John, named after his dad, John Chambliss."

No one with so much as a sideways glance at another. Finally, Bondi raised a hand.

"What can we do for you, boss?"

"Bondi, you and the posse can hold down the fort while I saddle up and go scout for the renegade."

Chapter Twenty

Across the street and one door down from Julio's was a house under renovation with a ten-yard dumpster at the curb. It was filled to the brim with mold-infested Sheetrock and rotted studs and the other detritus of a long-neglected rental finally busted down to uninhabitable.

Jeep had parked the Tahoe on the far side behind it and facing away and so hidden from anyone arriving to, departing from, or hanging out in Julio's house. He had positioned the driver's side-view mirror to frame the yard, porch and front door of Julio's house. He'd brought compact field glasses that, when focused on the lunchroom tray–size side mirror, gave an aspect that jumped it from Objects Are Closer Than They Appear to a full-on IMAX Experience.

Jeep's cell phone buzzed and lit up with Coach's digits.

"Hey, Coach."

"Yeah hey, that address I gave you is out of date. Julio moved a couple months ago," he said.

"Ahhhh, shit . . ."

"But that's not the thing. I just called Julio to confirm the new address 'cause I all of a sudden had a pang, these guys do tend to move around and I didn't want another fuck-up with you—"

Jeep moved him along, "What's the thing?"

"Mateo got on and asked if I knew a guy named 'Jeep.' Said this kid staying with them was told to find 'Jeep.'"

"Told by who?"

"Didn't say."

"Kid's name Angel?"

"Yeah. But he's gone from them a half hour ago, on his way out of town. Meeting his ride at the 7-Eleven in Glen Cove."

"Which 7-Eleven? There's three."

"Good point. He didn't say."

"Call 'em back, see if they know."

"You got it," Coach said, and hung up.

Jeep started the Tahoe and pulled a fast U-turn and floored it past the house he'd wasted three hours watching.

Jeep figured his best bet was the 7-Eleven in the strip mall off Water Street where he'd sent Diaz to canvass early that morning. The lot was mostly empty, save for some beer-and-cigarettes runners at the 7-Eleven and a few night owls at the Spanish-signage laundromat next door. Jeep parked in the half dark between the sodium-vapor security streetlights, doing his best to stay invisible in his shiny Tahoe and khaki uniform and thinking *good luck with that*.

His phone buzzed with a text. They don't know which one, from Coach. Jeep tried not to let this get to him.

A Dodge Caravan rolled in and parked in the half dark twenty yards over. No one got out to buy beer and cigarettes or do laundry.

Jeep slouched down some and trained the field glasses on the 7-Eleven windows and realized that both the patrons and the employees were young and Hispanic. He tried not to let this get to him, either.

A Volkswagen GTI announced itself with the bark of aftermarket exhaust and slid into a slot just ahead of the Dodge. It had Connecticut plates, which, given the time and place, Jeep filed as unlikely to match the registration of the car they were screwed onto. No one got out.

A while went by, enough time for Jeep to realize he had one shot and one shot only. If a young Hispanic male walked into the 7-Eleven and another one got out of the GTI or the Caravan or both, then the young male inside was Angel.

More time went by, enough for Jeep to add up all the Hail Mary aspects of his plan. A couple Slim Jims started a fire in the pit of his stomach.

A young Hispanic male in a backward ball cap rolled up on a junker banana-seat bike and leaned it against the glass and went in.

As another young Hispanic male got out of the back seat of the Caravan, and another from the shotgun seat of the GTI.

As Jeep turned the ignition, hit the lights and sirens, shot across the lot and stopped sharply ten feet from the door, front wheels up on the sidewalk. He jumped out and ran into the 7-Eleven and came up fast behind the male.

"Police! Get on the ground! NOW!"

The male dropped to the floor. Jeep dropped to a knee and patted him up and down and leaned in and said, real low, "*Soy* Jeep. *Manos detras de tu espalda.*"

He obeyed, putting his hands behind his back as Jeep got his cuffs out and snapped them on, noticing the vintage Rolex Daytona on the kid's wrist.

Jeep hauled him to his feet and turned him around. He had his mother's height, about five-eight, but he looked more like his father with each passing year.

Jeep ducked him in the back seat of the Tahoe and fastened the seat belt. He closed the door and walked around the back to check the coast.

Three of the younger guys and a middle-aged one with a shaved head and tears tattooed under one eye stood sulking by their rides, half hidden in the shadows. If they were cartoons, they'd be the jackals or hyenas with the glowing eyes in a Disney classic that gives the littler kids nightmares.

Jeep shot them a salute, got in and drove off.

"I speak English," Angel said.

"Good for you," Jeep said.

"I just mean, if it's easier."

"Where'd you get the watch?" Jeep said.

"My father gave it to me."

"*Gave* it."

"Yeah. It went from his grandfather to his father to him to me."

Which would have to have been explained to him by Johnny. Only Payson "Pace" Chambliss's name was inscribed on the back; the lineage would have to be filled in by someone who knew it, you couldn't just look at the back of the watch and read it.

Jeep played his ace regardless.

"But you killed him anyway?" Jeep said.

Jeep's eyes went back and forth from road ahead to rearview mirror in split-second shifts. He'd turned the back-seat dome light on and had a clear view. Angel's face twisted.

"He's dead?"

"Like you didn't know?"

Jeep had seen it too many times, notifying the next of kin. That moment when all the natural defenses collapse in an instant, when it hits them that *it must be true, why else would a stranger be telling me this?* The shock to the system, the primeval howl, the muscles and equilibrium giving way and the collapse to the sidewalk or the floor. He'd seen a few persons of interest try to fake it, and one in particular deserved an Oscar. But within ten seconds, you could tell whose deal was real and whose was just an epically cynical dodge.

For Angel, the tell was the gush of tears and snot as he rocked back and forth, bound in his seat. If you're really good, you can fake tears. But he'd never seen someone fake the snot bubbling out the nose and soaking the wispy mustache.

"Me kill him? Nooooooo, no no no . . ." With genuine, chaotic anguish.

"You didn't know," Jeep said.

"No, I didn't know," Angel said.

"I'm sorry," Jeep said. Like he meant it, because he did.

"It's like. The opposite. *He saved. My life.*" Talking in bites, trying to get his breath back, all the fluids choking him up.

Jeep pulled a quick right into the CW Post campus entrance. He pulled into a visitor's lot, out of sight from Northern Boulevard, and put the Tahoe in park. He got out and released Angel's seat belt and leaned him forward and unlocked the handcuffs and reached the bandanna in his back pocket and handed it to the kid.

"This is called a prisoner release. I arrested you by mistake. You are free to go. Do you understand what I have told you?"

"Yes."

Angel got out and wiped down his face and blew his nose and turned over the bandanna and blew it again.

"Why did you arrest me?"

"Because I'm pretty sure the guys you were meeting for a ride were going to kill you. We know they've been looking for you all week."

He shook his head and kicked at the asphalt.

"I was promised I could trust them."

"Then you got a beef with whoever. My money's on that Mateo, he mentioned me by name."

"You saying you saved my life?"

"Well, extended it by a day or two, maybe. They'll be tracking you."

"So, I'm free to go *where?*"

He'd dried up, tears and snot-wise, but he still had the look of a crushed eight-year-old boy.

"Well, Angel, that's up to you. But I will tell you, that boatyard's under watch now."

The kid's reaction confirming his recent campsite.

"My name is Juan."

"Why they call you Angel?"

"The gang tags you when you come in."

"Why Angel?"

"The boss gives the tags. He's a *maricon*. He said I was pretty so I could go by Angel or Shakira. I took Angel."

"Got it," Jeep said. "And who told you to find me?"

"My father. He said if we got separated and he couldn't reach me to find Jeep and I said why does it matter what car and he said no, Jeep is a man, our family's best friend."

"Then why didn't you?"

"'Cause he said you were a cop. Sorry."

There was nothing in any Patrol Guide for this. Jeep tried to channel his dad but there was way too much static. He was on his own.

"A cop who has to get back to work. Drop you somewhere?"

"Like, *where*?"

"What're you saying, Juan?"

"I need help."

"I look like the Red Cross?"

"My father said you were the family's best friend."

Jeep saw the crack in the door, got a toe in.

"Friendship with your family has always been kind of transactional."

"What's that mean?"

"You do something for me, I do something for you."

Which would, actually, hold up in court. An honest account by an honest cop, no coercion in sight.

"What could I do for you?" Juan said.

"Ride up front with me while I make a couple calls."

• • •

Jeep made three calls. The first was to Assistant District Attorney D'Andre Tomlinson, who he'd known since they were teenagers when Tomlinson played lacrosse for Manhasset and drew comparisons to the legendary Jim Brown, partly for his speed and stamina but also for being a Black kid in a historically white kid's sport. He'd brought the speed and stamina to the DA's office and added a knack for finding the "common good."

The second call was to Alana Wertheimer, who was the sleekest shark in the County Public Defender's Office. Alana was the daughter of a wealthy Garden City orthodontist and had a law degree from Harvard but was working out some self-worth issues toiling for the County and was well known, and loathed by cops, as a rabid zealot for the underdog criminal classes.

The third call was to Detective Arbogast, partly out of respect for protocol but partly to lord shit over him, should things go as Jeep hoped they would.

Jeep had apologized to all three for the late hour but had stressed that the matter was of urgent importance to a critical and ongoing County problem. All three bit, though with some harsh words for him.

Those three, plus Juan, were still hashing out the borders and boundaries in the little conference room in C Trailer as Jeep paid the DoorDash guy for the two pizzas and liter of Coke. It was just past midnight when he brought in the pies and the Coke.

"What do we got?" Jeep said. He put one pie in front of Juan, who inhaled a slice as he reached for a second.

"Kind of a gold mine, this holds up." Arbogast tucked a corner of paper towel under his collar, old-school bib, and reached for the box.

Alana took this as her cue to caution against assumptions. Anytime a cop opens his mouth she takes as her cue to caution against assumptions.

"My client is not admitting to any criminal activity, nor has he been charged with any. He is, however, willingly and knowingly offering to testify, with eyewitness accounts and including times, dates, names, addresses and phone numbers, his accounts of the criminal activities of the Cruceros, a car-theft syndicate operating in the County."

"What's Cruceros?" Jeep said to Juan.

"The Cruisers, that's what they call themselves," Juan said through a mouthful.

"In exchange for?" Jeep asked.

"Immunity and protection," Alana said.

"Protection, how?" Jeep said.

"Secured transport to Cabo San Lucas, Mexico, where his uncle has a room for him and a job at his steakhouse," Tomlinson said.

"Yeah, valet parking," Arbogast said, dry as a bone. Everyone laughed, including Juan.

Tomlinson looked from Alana to Juan. "All of which will have to be verified up the wazoo."

"I already talked to him," Juan said.

"Agreed," Alana said.

"Who's got his phone?" Jeep asked.

"The fishes," Juan said. "That's how they were tracking me, so I threw it in the sea."

Alana said, "But he says he saved everything to the Cloud."

"I don't just say that, I did that. For *insurance*," Juan said, feisty.

"Abundance of caution, I'm going to get a warrant," Tomlinson said. He nodded toward Alana. "I'll have it by nine so say nine fifteen, my office, to tape his deposition?"

"Works for me," Alana said.

"Works for me," Arbogast said.

"I'll have him there," Jeep said.

"You're not placing him in protective custody?" Alana said.

"I am. With me. I'll have him there at nine fifteen."

Alana and Tomlinson exchanged a look, started packing up their briefcases. Juan reached a third slice. Arbogast leaned in to Jeep.

"You reach out to the PC?"

"No, I thought that'd be your job, as his lead investigator."

"I'm lead investigator on the DOA."

"Which also bore this fruit here, wouldn't you say?"

"Kind of a stretch," Arbogast said.

"This kid's not here without your help. You should walk it in. Knight wouldn't like it if the intel came from a banger flipped by Andy of Mayberry."

"What do you care what Knight likes?"

"I don't, personally. But him owing me a solid is good for business, you're a Chief of Police around here."

Arbogast looked at Jeep like waiting for the tell; the pulling on an earlobe, the jiggling knee. None came.

Arbogast said, "We'll walk him in together."

Sergeant Bondurant had a small ranch house on a half acre overlooking the Sound out past the Target Rock Wildlife Refuge on Lloyd Neck, which was the end of the earth on the North Shore. Out of an abundance of caution Jeep had asked Bondi if he and Juan could crash there for the night, Jeep's own home in Bayville being too close to the past week's action for comfort. Plus, it gave Bondi a role he was born to play, that of the Lawman setting in the rocker outside the sheriff's office, finger on the trigger of the hogleg in his lap, eyes peeled for bushwhackers and sidewinders. Or, for Juan, should he have hornswoggled them all and tried to vamoose.

The house was about a forty-minute drive from the station. Juan started yawning the moment Jeep started the Tahoe. Jeep poked him in the ribs, not gently.

"What?" Juan said.

"Wake the fuck up."

"What did I do?"

"No, it's what *didn't* you do, yet."

"What?"

"Tell me what happened last Saturday night."

Chapter Twenty-One

Juan had gotten Johnny's cell number from his mother after a long, tearful call where he told her he was giving up gang life and coming home. He promised he wouldn't ask his father for a single peso; he just wanted to meet him. Between the tears and the wheedling he finally crowbarred it out of her with an additional promise not to tell Johnny that his mother had never married and still worked at the resort. Instead, she told Juan to just describe her dream for her life: a rich American had fallen for her and even moved there for her and they lived like a king and his queen on their vast cattle ranch near the Argentine border.

Juan had almost given up hope when Johnny finally appeared at the beach.

"Hey," his father said, from a ways away.

"Hey."

"How you doing?"

"Okay. Thanks for coming."

"Last time I saw you, you were eight."

His father had held out a palm, estimating height.

"What do you mean, saw me?"

"On the soccer field, a game after school."

"You came all the way to see me play?"

"Well, yeah. Just to see . . ." His father broke off, like maybe he was unsure of how to explain that hour from a decade ago.

"Did I score?"

"Yeah. Beautiful goal. Maybe two, I can't remember exactly."

"I was always a defender. I hardly ever shot, never scored." Juan had sworn he wouldn't try to bust him about anything but there it was.

"Oh," his father said after an awkward moment, then tried to recover with "Truth be told I was just watching your face, through binoculars, trying to see what you looked like, but you on the run turning this way and that, fifty yards away, so you know, the game itself kind of a blur."

Exactly none of this was going according to the movie Juan had played over and over in his head the last years. Where his father took him in a big hug and tried to hold back tears and kept taking Juan's face in his hands and marveling at it. Where the boy and his father played "favorite things" and couldn't believe how much they had in common, from food to music to sports to automobiles to hating church except on Christmas. Where after an hour or so of nonstop talking they just sat side by side and looked out at the same road or sea or horizon together and were silent, just so at peace, finally in each other's company.

"So, what brings you up here?" his father asked.

"I steal expensive cars, for a crew, for money."

"Wow," his father said, like he was trying to find some fatherly pride but couldn't, quite.

"But I quit."

"Probably for the best, huh?"

Juan started to wonder what his mother ever saw in this guy. He was handsome, sure, and apparently rich, or was when she met him. But he seemed so unsure of himself, even just in an everyday give-and-take.

"They let you just, like, resign from that?"

"No, they be looking for me. And not to throw me a, you know, farewell party. I've got a flight to Los Angeles tomorrow night, then down to Cabo San Lucas."

"I've been there! Beautiful country!"

"My uncle has a restaurant I can work in. Gotta lay low for a while."

"Can I give you a hug?" his father said, throwing Juan a little.

"Sure."

His father stepped up to him and hugged him tight. When they broke he noticed his father wipe away tears with the back of his hand.

"Sorry. Kind of . . . emotional. Not trying to embarrass you."

"No worries."

A few frames of the movie Juan had imagined had just played.

"I got five hundred from the ATM, that's all they let you take out."

"I don't need money."

"C'mon, tide you over."

"No, but thank you."

"Well, you gotta take this."

He took off his wristwatch and held it out.

"I can't, really."

"No, I mean, you *got to*. It's a tradition in my family. My grandfather to my father at eighteen then to me at eighteen and now to you. You are eighteen, right?"

"Yeah, but—"

"Then you gotta."

His father took Juan's hand and put the old watch in it and Juan shrugged and slipped it on his wrist but couldn't figure out the clasp and his father showed him how.

"It's called a Daytona, this is the like, earliest one. Worth some real money."

"I'm not gonna sell it."

"Keep it, sell it, I don't care. It's been passed down by sons of bitches, maybe you *should* sell it and not become one."

His father smiled, a great American smile full of white teeth and mischief, like the actor Jack Nicholson flashed when he was his father's age. Juan smiled too.

"You think it's cursed?"

"Could be. Wear it for a while, see if you turn into a total asshole." They laughed.

"How's your mother?" his father asked.

"You want her version or the real one."

"How about both."

"She lives on a huge ranch with a man who loves her more every day and has piles of money. Or, she still works in the hotel where you met her but she's a manager now and she has an okay boyfriend and worries about me so much she gets stomachaches, she says."

His father didn't say anything for a minute, just looked out at the sea and then slipped his jacket off.

"It's so hot for September," his father said.

"I don't know, I've only been here a couple weeks."

"Let's go for a swim. Water's great."

"No, thanks."

"C'mon . . ." His father looked at him like it was important.

"I can't swim."

"Well, I can. So I'll teach you."

By then he had stripped down to his boxers and was wrapping it all up in a bundle.

"We won't go any farther than where you can still stand, I promise."

He walked over to the rock jetty and stowed the clothes and shoes in a gap.

"Juan, I am your father and I am asking just this one thing. Let me teach you how to swim?"

There was a tone in his voice like this was urgent to him with a backbeat of *please don't say no*.

But what Juan said was "FUCK!"

"WHAT?!" his father said.

Juan shoved his hands in his pockets and came out with a cell phone from the front pocket and a small black fabric bag from the back.

"I forgot to put it back in the bag," Juan said, agitated.

"What bag?"

"Faraday bag, blocks the satellites or whatever from showing where you are. Fuck!"

Juan held out a hand, signaling for silence and stillness.

He looked west. A car was circling the parking lot of the public beach just over, headlights on high beam. You could hear voices calling back and forth in Spanish between the car and a man jogging on the beach.

"They may have tracked me," Juan said.

"Who?" his father said.

"Los Cruceros. The gang. Get your clothes, we gotta—"

They noticed headlights cutting the dark maybe fifty yards up from them. Two pairs, two cars pulling up hot. Four car doors slamming in succession. Flashlight beams playing off the wood shingles of the cabanas.

Juan was frozen. His father grabbed him by the arm and pulled him to the water. Juan was terrified. He really did not know how to swim and so had a great fear of big bodies of water and drowning in one. His father grabbed his hand and pulled him with surprising strength. They waded as silently as they could, until the water was up to Juan's waist.

"Get on my back," his father whispered as he stretched out. Juan got his arms around his father's neck. His father pushed off and stroked, heading out.

Between the arcs of his strokes with his arms and his frog kicks with his legs it was hard for Juan to hold on. He panicked, starting to slip off, clawing at his father's wet and slippery back, tearing up the skin with his long, unclipped nails. His father hissed some pain but spoke to him in a low and even voice.

"Easy, easy. It's just a piggyback ride."

Which gave Juan some comfort and direction and he got his arms around his father's chest and clasped his hands together and laid his head sideways between his father's shoulder blades.

"Kick a little, out the sides," his father said, his breath coming hard.

Juan did, flailing at first, but then settling into a rhythm with his father, pitching in.

Juan could hear the Cruceros on the beach calling out his name with command at first and then, mockingly, like they were calling a dog.

Either they gave up or Juan and his father were out of earshot, and all he could hear was his father's labored breathing and the small splashes as they plowed along.

After a while his father headed into shore, toward a long crescent of beach with a big old shingled building as the hub of some smaller ones. Off to the left some boat shapes shone in the moonlight, shrink-wrapped in white plastic; ghost ships.

His father gently pulled Juan's hands apart but held on to one. The water only came up to his waist. They waded toward shore. Juan saw that his father's back was bleeding.

"I scratched your back up. I'm sorry."

"I can barely feel it, no worries."

They sat on the beach, breathing hard for a minute. His father stretched out his arms and shoulders, arcing side to side. Then he pointed toward the white boats.

"Hide up there, I'll come find you."

"Where you going?" Panic creeping up on Juan again.

"I'm gonna swim back and get my clothes and my phone and call Jeep."

"Call a Jeep?" Juan said, with confusion on top of panic.

"No, Jeep. It's the name of a friend of mine. He's a good cop, he can find the bad guys. Make us safe. You're ever in trouble around here you call Jeep. He's our family's best friend."

Juan thought this Jeep sounded like a character in a Marvel or DC comic.

"You hide in the boats, I'll be back in a half hour or so. I'll be in a Defender, you know what that is?"

"Range Rover."

"Mine's an old one."

"You can really swim back?"

"Without you for a knapsack? Shit, yeah."

His father smiled that smile again. It made Juan feel hopeful for the first time in a long time.

"What if they're still there?"

"Then they'll see some crazy gringo went for a night swim, no?"

"They're bad guys."

His father reached out and ruffed the boy's hair.

"And they've definitely moved on still looking for you so go hide already, I'll see you in a few."

His father stretched his arms one more time and stood up and waded into the water and dove in. He swam much faster alone, slicing through the dark water with long strokes and strong, even kicks. Juan watched him for a few moments then took his phone and although it was likely dead from drowning he flung it into the water, just to be safe. He walked toward the boats.

He'd picked his hiding place and was about to crawl in when he heard a mechanical whine from the water and scooted over to the pylon by the dock to have a look. There were two of them on those water motorcycles, whatever they're called, making tight circles. He panicked again, wondering if he'd missed something, wondering if Los Cruceros had some kind of navy at their command. But then the water motorcycles slowed down and drifted together, and he relaxed when he heard two American teenage-boy voices giving each other shit and laughing it up. One of them had a sound system on board and thumping hip-hop started up and then they gunned their machines and disappeared and the night was over for Juan except for the waiting for his father.

Chapter Twenty-Two

Officer Diaz and Corporal Jackson arrived just after seven the next morning with a suit, shirt and shoes of Diaz's for Juan and traditional Lawn Guyland breakfasts for all: bacon egg and cheese salt pepper ketchup on a Kaiser roll, plus coffees in tall cardboard cups. They ate on Bondi's patio overlooking the Sound as the sun struggled up over striated clouds to the east, and when they were done Juan was sent off with the clothes and a razor and instructions to make himself look like a young man with a bright future.

Jeep debriefed his three officers on Juan's account of The Night Of and sent them off to meet Arbogast and the county's CSU and Forensics teams at the Bridge Marina in Bayville. He'd called and downloaded Arbogast at one that morning after Juan had finished his account and he'd pointed out to Arbogast that the Dead in Dead on Arrival were due a record of the means and methods by which they Arrived. Arbogast agreed to revisit the marinas and coordinate the search for the Sea-Doo or Yamaha or Kawasaki that likely tore off Johnny's face.

"You gonna be there?" Arbogast had said.

"Soon as I drop the kid," Jeep had said.

"Since when do we call gangbangers 'kids'?"

"Sorry. Soon as I drop the *worthless piece of shit*."

"That's more like it," Arbogast had said.

He had a point, Jeep thought. A first cousin of the same point Johnny had made when Jeep had graduated onto the Job; that Jeep was deficient in the harsh and deeply cynical nature it took to succeed as a cop. And here it was fifteen years later and he was calling this remorseless car thief and certified burden on society a *what*? A "kid," like he was some hot-hand pitching prospect from the boonies.

When Juan came back out a half hour later, time collapsed for a moment as Jeep was reunited with Johnny at age eighteen. Well, Johnny with a deep tan and wearing a suit the real Johnny wouldn't be caught dead in, but still. Juan was clean-shaven, hair slicked back showing the hereditary Chambliss widow's peak, and with a smile that aimed at confidence but wavered well short of it, as his father's did if you knew how to look. Juan held out a striped tie.

"I never learned this," he said.

"Here."

Jeep turned him around and flipped up the shirt collar and tied a four-in-hand and turned him back around and snugged the knot. He held the tie up and turned it inside out.

"Now, most guys slip the thin end into this loop here to keep the two ends in one straight line but your father always kept it loose 'cause he thought it was cooler that way."

Juan inspected the tie situation, slipped the thinner end into the Perry Ellis–branded loop and buttoned the jacket.

"Not trying to be cool today."

"Just so's you know."

Juan reached a frayed ballistic nylon wallet from his pocket and dug out a card and handed it to Jeep. It was a dollar-off coupon from a pizza parlor in Oyster Bay and had the soft wrinkled aspect of having been soaked wet and then dried.

"Other side," Juan said.

On the back were a set of numbers and degree symbols in a geographic coordinate, still legible, though blurred a little fuzzy.

"That's for you," Juan said.

"What's for me?"

"The . . . thing that's there."

"Speak English, please?"

"You don't want me to, trust me," Juan said.

"I *don't* trust you. I'm a cop and you're a car thief."

Arbogast might have punctuated it with a backhand to the ear with his fat dive watch, but Jeep was satisfied just to draw the line and the kid did look stung.

"It was gonna be my, like, insurance. I can't use it now and maybe you'd like it as a thank-you for maybe saving my ass. That's all I'm gonna say."

Jeep drove Juan to the District Attorney's office in Mineola and delivered him up to the third-floor conference room where Tomlinson and Wertheimer were already ensconced with audio and video equipment and a Tech Unit officer to run them and a stenographer to take a transcript. On the ride over, Juan had panicked some as his frame of reference for interrogations ran to legends from back home of cigarette burns and cattle prods. Jeep stayed through the taped self-introductions, the date and time, the dotted *i*'s and crossed *t*'s of the terms of Juan's cooperation.

He caught Juan's eye and gestured as if asking for his permission to go, and got it.

Corporal Jackson was the only cop left at the Bridge Marina when Jeep got there. She was securing yellow crime-scene tape across a finger pier where a half dozen jet skis were up on floating docks.

"What do we got?" Jeep said as he approached. The wind had come up, the plastic tape snapped and fluttered.

"They took some samples they liked off to the lab, well, I shouldn't say liked, but thought might be human hair samples in that Sea-Doo I think in the well of the tread wheel underneath that drives these things."

Quick as the speeded-up legalese at the end of a radio ad for prescription drugs, as always.

"Detective Arbogast?" Jeep said.

"Ran the tags on these jet skis and headed to the addresses to canvass the owners as to the boats' whereabouts on The Night Of two from Mill Neck one from Centre Island three from here in Bayville."

So a fifty percent chance local rich kid Johnny Careless was run over by another careless local rich kid, Jeep thought. Jeep hated irony, thought it was a cheap and snarky way of processing life's heartbreakingly rich pageant.

"Bondi post you?"

"'Til they get the warrants and the flatbed comes for the jet skis of interest."

"You want a coffee or anything?"

"I'm good but thanks, and, boss, I hope they do find something and ID whoever did this even if it was a stupid kid thought they hit a log just so's you can have closure on your friend," Jackson said.

"Thank you, Corporal. Appreciate that."

The blurred-ink coordinates on the back of the dollar-off pizza coupon dropped Jeep at the Town of Oyster Bay Highway Operations lot just north of the Expressway in Syosset. As he didn't know what he was looking for he couldn't spot it outright and as it was gifted, if that was the word, by a car-jacking undocumented immigrant, he didn't want to make an inquiry at the front desk. So he cruised the vast lot in a grid and rolled some calls, the first couple to Bondi and Diaz for updates, the third to Arbogast.

"It's Chief Mullane, what do we got?"

"They sent the preliminary samples over to the ME and we're waiting on if there's a match or if it's just flotsam or jetsam, I guess. They got the jet skis on a truck, and, hold on—"

Arbogast interrupted himself with a loud eruption and, from the sound of it, hawked an epic gob of phlegm.

"Sorry. There's two kids live in big-ass Mill Neck houses I'm gonna swing back over and interview when they get home from practice."

"Because?" Jeep asked.

"Because surveillance footage at the marina has the two kids, in wet-suits, getting in a BMW X5 at eleven forty-eight on Saturday night and the tags on the car register back to the same address as the tags on two of the jet skis. That good enough for you, Chief?"

Just then Jeep saw what he didn't know he was looking for.

"Ten-four," he said, and hung up.

In a far corner of the vast lot, to the right of a huge corrugated-tin shed and just past the fleet of salt spreaders, loomed two mounds of sand and rock salt, each a couple stories high, like scale versions of the mountain formations that always get named Camelback.

Jeep drove over and parked past the fleet. If you wanted to hide something, with easy and anonymous access to that something's retrieval, the salt and sand piles stored for winter's road maintenance likely went unchecked in late September. He made his way behind the mounds and toward the chain-link fenced border of the yard and there it was, wearing a sagging one-size-fits-most AutoZone cover.

Mayor Mark LaSalle had to pass on Jeep's urgent summons as he was in Chicago on business. Mayors Chaz Scarborough, Maisie Coffin and Walter Donahue had replied that they would rearrange their schedules and gather at Centre Brookville PD headquarters at four. Jeep had called up his scheduled night-shift officers and promised them three hours at

the overtime buffet to come in early, in uniform, and line up in formation in the HQ parking lot. Donahue had arrived last, still driving his
Porsche Gold Coast courtesy vehicle. He got out, looked around, and
stepped up to Jeep.

"Okay, what is this?"

"This is the Village of Centre Brookville Police Department, in formation," Jeep said.

"And I'm a busy man," Donahue replied. He gestured to his fellow
mayors and generously added, "As are Chaz and Maisie."

"And we appreciate your taking the time," Jeep said.

A radio crackled with some staticky report; Corporal Jackson re-
layed the message to Jeep.

"About three minutes out," she said.

"What is?" Donahue demanded.

Jeep walked over to the lineup of officers.

"Ten-hut!" he barked, and they all snapped to attention, saluting.

"As you were," Jeep said.

They dropped their salutes but remained at attention as Jeep turned
back and addressed the mayors.

"The cop walking the beat or driving on patrol is invisible to the
people. How can that *be*, you might ask. He or she is in uniform, wears
a shield, carries a weapon, drives around in a vehicle equipped with
lights and sirens and more signage than a NASCAR Chevy. But they
are . . . *invisible*. You don't see them. Who they are, how and why they
came to wear that uniform. You don't see the fear, the doubt, the nerve
endings frayed by all the adrenaline surges. You don't see the wrecked
livers and burning ulcers that come with going out every day and night
to engage with the very worst in human behavior, or to mop up after
all the heartbreaking tragedies God sends our way. So be it. That's what
we signed up for. That's what we call the Job."

Jeep sensed a stirring in the ranks behind him. Public attaboys were rare in day-to-day suburban policing, especially ones as purple as the Chief was doling out. Their collective stance grew a little taller, a little straighter.

Jeep heard the shriek and pop of the powerful engine approaching.

"But once in a while the cops have a victory that is crystal clear to the public and so a cause for celebration. The puppy rescued, the hostage released unharmed, the armed robbery that ends without a single shot being fired."

By this point, Donahue and the other two mayors were looking at Jeep like he'd burst into flames.

Jeep's timing was a couple beats short of the actual arrival, but the alarming scream of the engine at the redline functioned as trumpets blaring the announcement.

Diaz drifted the Paint to Sample Irish Green Porsche Targa 4S into the lot and jerked the wheel hard as he braked and the car slid sideways to a stop barely six feet from the Mayors.

"Mayor Donahue, your ride's here," Jeep said.

"Oh my God," Donahue said, genuinely moved.

Diaz popped out and joined the ranks.

Donahue hovered over the car, touching it lightly, leaning in close and murmuring softly, like he wanted to cradle it in his arms and kiss its forehead.

"Courtesy of the hard work, bravery and dedication of your Centre Brookville PD. Who *surely* deserve a round of applause."

Jeep gestured to the formation like a ringmaster to the daredevils. His dad had always advised, "Never waste an opportunity to overpraise your fellow cops."

Chaz and Maisie started clapping hard and fast and Donahue joined in and added some "hell yeahs!" to the mix and the troops broke out in grins.

· · ·

By the time Jeep got back to Mineola to collect Juan from his deposition, Arbogast was already there, sitting in the lobby and playing Hearts with an app on his phone. Jeep took the chair next to him.

"What do we got?"

"They need another five or so with him."

"And the Jet Ski Killers?"

Arbogast laughed, shrugged.

"One Conor Geddes and one Liam Wellington, both seventeen, both admitted to being out on them after dark, which is of course against the law. Said they were clean and sober, no way to know otherwise, but no records, either of them, suggesting otherwise. And they did have safety certification, so not even a Brianna's Law violation. The Geddes kid thought he hit a log or a dolphin."

"You believe him?"

"He actually could've, nothing's come back positive from the lab yet. And yeah, I believe him."

Arbogast inspected Jeep with a sidelong look.

"You got a reason I shouldn't?" Arbogast said.

"No."

"Being typical private school dipshits is all they're guilty of far as I can tell, but maybe you want to interview them yourself."

"It is what it is, I guess," Jeep said.

Being careless wasn't a crime around there, just a tribal custom.

"They're juniors at Shelter Rock and they're both on the lacrosse team," Arbogast said.

Jeep shot him a look but before he could follow up Arbogast put a hand on his shoulder.

"I don't know you well but I think I know you well enough to know you'd wanna know."

He was right, Jeep thought.

"I hate irony."

"Who the fuck hates irony? What a waste of time," Arbogast said, making a face.

"Why's that?"

"I mean, save hate for the shit you can avoid, like, I don't know, chain Mexican or carpet shopping. You can't avoid irony, *it* finds *you*, whenever it wants."

Jeep tried to parse the logic.

"You don't *hate* Lou Gehrig's disease? I mean, you couldn't avoid it, your wife got it?"

"Oh, I do, with a fucking passion. But it would only be *ironic* if my wife played first base for the Yankees."

Jeep parsed a little more, then chalked one up for Arbogast as he typed his response to a text on his cell phone.

"They're ready for us," Arbogast said.

"What's the plan?"

"We hand off Juan to the PC and his chiefs at seven, they get their downloads then sock him in an airport hotel with a sitter 'til his flight to L.A. in the morning."

In the few moments Jeep had had for spacing out in the past thirty-six hours, his mind had wandered to Niven. Specifically, to whether or not a call or text was in order, if only to bring her up to speed. But if Jeep was being honest with himself, which tortured him when it came to his feelings for her and had for more than half his life, he knew that the call or text would be in fact a pretext. For a chance to listen closely for intimate inflection or a left-field double entendre, or to track the flow of the texts for a hairpin turn to chances of last-minute, late-night drinks. Honestly, for any crumb or hint or whiff that might signal that his complicated longing was a condition she shared.

It was exhausting and distracting work, all that, and he blamed it for taking his eyes off the prize.

He checked his watch and calculated time and distance.

"Push to eight."

"You don't push the PC. Even you know that."

"It's non-negotiable." Backed up with one of Jeep's neutral-aggressive deadpans. "I've got to push."

"For what?"

"It's a family matter," Jeep said.

Chapter Twenty-Three

Pete Chambliss had two decades-long standing reservations at the Two Trees Club; the first was his eight-forty Sunday morning tee time after the early service at St. Luke's and the second was at seven sharp on Friday evenings at the table just right of the fireplace in the upstairs dining room in the Clubhouse. This allowed time for cocktails to be ordered and delivered, menus reviewed and choices noted, plus ample time for table-hopping before the starters were laid down at precisely seven twenty-five.

Jeep and Juan were on the long drive that bordered the first and second holes by seven twenty. Jeep hated to do it this way, it stunk of grandstanding, but the timing being what it was he had no choice.

Jeep parked close to the main entrance, in a spot strictly reserved for the current club president, flaunting the bylaws. They got out of the Tahoe, and Jeep did a quick inspection and pushed the kid's hair back and straightened his tie.

"What do I call them?" Juan asked.

"Grammy and Poppy'd be fun," Jeep said.

"Really?"

"No. Mr. and Mrs. Chambliss," Jeep said.

They walked inside and up the stairs and past the coatroom and stopped just inside the dining room. Two of the ever-vigilant waitstaff noticed them and looked to each other for guidance as the nearby tables ceased their yakking and gawked. In the dining room at Two Trees, a uniformed Chief of Police and a long-haired Chilean car thief wearing a super-slim burgundy suit were about as inconspicuous as the two surviving Beatles strolling in.

With all the authority vested in him, Jeep took Juan by the arm and marched him across the room toward the fireplace.

Gwen saw them first and froze for the instant it took her to understand what was happening. Then, she put her napkin aside and rose to her feet as Pete looked up at her and she held out a hand for him to rise as well and he looked and saw what was coming and frowned and stayed seated.

She said, "Manners," and stuck a knuckle in his shoulder. Pete stood as Jeep and Juan arrived.

"Pete and Gwen, this is Juan Soto. Juan, Mr. and Mrs. Chambliss," Jeep said, deciding on an all-purpose intro.

Neither had to say "I feel like I've seen a ghost"; it was all over their faces. Juan looked to Jeep, as if for his cue. Jeep just jerked his head and Juan got it.

"Nice to meet you," Juan said.

"And you, Juan," Gwen said, managing a smile and extending her hand, which Juan gently shook.

"May we join you for a moment?" Jeep said.

"Of course," Pete managed, and they all sat. A waitress appeared at the table.

"May I—"

Jeep cut her off quickly, politely. "Thank you, we're not staying."

Pete looked slightly relieved. Gwen passed the breadbasket to Juan, who took a square of focaccia and bit off half as he passed the basket to Jeep, who waved it away.

Jeep said, "We only have a minute; I'm delivering Juan to County detectives and they're putting him on a plane in the morning."

"Where are you headed?" Gwen said. Brightly, like she might have restaurant recommendations for him, covering for her sideways state of mind.

Jeep put a hand on Juan's arm, staying him.

"He can't say. He's flipping on a crew of car thieves that have been working our area. They know that he's with us and they're looking for him."

Juan put the focaccia on the table, his appetite suddenly gone. Jeep looked right at Pete.

"Your grandson here is a very brave young man. He's putting himself, and probably his family back home, in great danger by helping us."

In fact, the Nassau DA's office had already flown Catalina to Cabo San Lucas, but Jeep felt this territory had enough weeds as it was.

"Your grandson was with Johnny last Saturday night. Met his father for the first time, last Saturday night. And when it became apparent that this gang had tracked Juan and were on the attack, Johnny stepped up and saved his son's life. Turned out it was Johnny's last act on this earth. Your boy died saving his own boy."

Jeep felt he had every right and even duty to make sure the arrow was as sharp as it could be. Jeep knew he had this one shot to honor the legacy and character of his friend to that friend's dismissive and doubting father, and his aim had to be steady and true.

"Is this about money?" Pete said after a moment.

"Pete," Gwen said softly. "For God's sake."

"I'm sorry, but I have to live in the real world," Pete said.

Juan looked to Jeep. Jeep nodded.

"It was Jeep's idea, that you might want to meet me. I don't want money. I just went along for the ride."

Gwen said, "I'm so glad you went along, Juan. I'm so very happy to meet you."

Jeep wasn't quite done with Pete.

"Six days ago I came to your house to break the news that Johnny was dead. And when you saw me, you remember what you said?"

"I was in shock—"

"*Before* you knew," Jeep said. "You saw me and you said, 'The hell did he do now?'"

Pete Chambliss sat up straight in his chair and leaned forward, a man in full, fighting to the last.

"I loved my son. But, *and*, I knew him from the day he was born. And from the day he was born, he was trying to get back at me, and I never knew what for."

Pete Chambliss looked as close to crying as a man like him gets. Then he lost control, for once. He dabbed at his eyes with his napkin and gently waved his wife's hand away.

Juan poked Jeep with an elbow.

"We should go," Juan said.

"Yes, we should." Then, to Pete, "Look, I'm sorry, I didn't mean to . . ."

Pete just nodded quickly but had no words.

"I know you loved your son."

Gwen grabbed the wheel. "We know you loved our son, too. But that was pretty thoughtless of you. But there's been plenty of that to go around for way too long and there's no use pointing fingers anymore. He's gone and we all miss him and that's that."

Jeep looked at her in some wonder. Leave it to Gwen, he thought, a Queen of her tribe. With a wave of her hand she disarmed the table, like purposely knocking over her wineglass to ease an inebriated guest's embarrassment from knocking over his. It wasn't denial, it was her code of civility, and it had a peculiar grace.

She stood up abruptly. "Gerald, do you have your phone with you?"

"Yes, Mrs. Chambliss."

Turning back the clock with what they called each other. Whatever it took, Jeep thought.

"Would you take a picture of us with Juan?"

"Of course."

Gwen Chambliss patted her husband's back. He took a deep breath and stood, like her touch signaled *duty calls.* The tribe never shirked duty, even if it meant standing in front of the Two Trees dining room and posing with their bastard outlaw grandson for all the tribe to see.

Gwen held out a hand to Juan and he took it and she led him over to the fireplace and positioned him between her and Pete. They both put an arm around him and they both smiled like it was for the family Christmas card photograph, on top of Stratton Mountain or at the beach on Jupiter Island, because some things one just *does.*

Jeep and Juan rode up to the third floor with two uniformed officers who'd met them at the entrance. Arbogast was waiting for them outside the commissioner's conference room.

"What do we got?" Jeep said.

"NYPD, MTA, FBI, Jersey Staties and Newark PD. The band's all here, just waiting for the lead singer to show." He looked at Juan. "You ready, amigo?"

Juan said, "Sure," but his eyes were on Jeep and not so sure.

"Give me a second with him," Jeep said.

"You already pushed an hour," Arbogast complained.

Jeep flashed his watch and said, "Seven fifty-seven, so I got three minutes," and took Juan by the arm and walked him away.

"Your father saved your life so you owe him, right?" Jeep said, once they were out of earshot.

Juan had to think. Then he said, "I guess," but with some challenge in it.

"Yeah, you do. And all he'd want in return is for you to make this U-turn with your life. Help these cops with everything you have. Only way you'll ever really be free is if you turn your back on Los Cruceros.

And not for nothing, they were gonna kill you, so there's that too. Revenge. You want revenge, right?"

"I guess."

"You *guess*?"

"Well, they *didn't* kill me," Juan said.

Fucking teenagers, Jeep thought, and snapped at the kid.

"Oh, you'd rather have *proof* they'd kill you? You'd rather your mom got a picture of your corpse in her email? Then you'd have the clean conscience? That'd be too little too late, no?"

Juan recoiled, as Jeep had intended.

"You were on your way out anyway. Do some good with it. Comprende?"

"Si."

Jeep took the kid in a tight embrace and clapped him on the back.

"You take care, Juan."

"You too. And thank you, Jeep, thank you."

And finally, some genuine gratitude in the young man's tone.

"Showtime!" Arbogast called over.

Jeep walked Juan back. One of the uniforms opened the door to the conference room and the other one led Juan in and Jeep started for the elevator and Arbogast caught his sleeve.

"Hey, Chief, thanks," Arbogast said.

"Glad I could help."

"I could help you, too."

"You already did, Detective."

"Like if I put in my papers and was free to sign up with you."

Jeep looked at Arbogast, puzzled.

"Why would you do that?"

"I think that I could make you a sharper cop and that you could make me almost give a shit again."

He tapped Jeep on the shoulder and walked into the conference room.

• • •

Driving back up to the North Shore, Jeep wrestled with his conscience and lost the match. He could have carried out his duties that night without ambushing the Chamblisses at their club but he couldn't resist putting on the show. As much as he told himself that *in time they'll thank me* and *it's exactly what Johnny would have wanted*, he couldn't quite squirm out of the headlock. And slagging Pete Chambliss, to his face, in public, six days after his son's death? He could see his mother grimacing and his father shaking his head and swearing under his breath. He felt like all his better angels had taken the same night off.

He found himself turning onto the road that passed Niven's parents' house. It was, in fact, a shortcut back to Bayville, a rationale that lasted about a tenth of a mile. He wanted to see her, if only because her unselfconscious beauty and flinty sarcasm never failed to distract the shit out of him.

As he rounded the curve with the sign for their blind driveway he saw the Mercedes G-Wagen pulling out and accelerating toward him and flashing past, momentarily blinding him with its high beams. He realized that if she was heading to his house, she'd be driving in the other direction. You're better off, he told himself.

Just before he passed the house, he abruptly turned into the driveway and jumped on the brakes.

In the split second the Mercedes passed you could see the driver wore a hoodie, up. Niven doesn't wear hoodies.

And his headlights were shining on the very first aftermarket-tuned Volkswagen GTI that had ever been parked in the Belgian block circular driveway in front of Niven's parents' elegant 1930s Colonial.

He radioed in an alert on a green G-50 heading west on Hickory Tweed Lane and called for backup to number Thirty-six.

He got out of the Tahoe and got out his Glock 9mm and pushed the door gently shut and froze to listen to the night.

Chapter Twenty-Four

Some breeze in the trees, bringing a wet chill. The last of the birdsongs. Sweet smoke smell drifting down from a chimney.

The sound of shattering glass erupted from the mullioned bay window in the library wing at the west end of the house. Jeep bolted as he heard Niven's cry.

"HELP! SOMEBODY!"

He calculated in a flash; the window would have jagged shards and a four-foot climb. He grabbed the brass handle on the front door. Probably the one door that was locked. He stepped back and raised his right leg up and put all his weight into the kick and the door splintered off the frame and leaned inside. He stepped in and hung the left and bounded through the living room shouting: "POLICE!"

He pulled up fast and got an eye around the jamb and into the room.

A small fire smoldered in the fireplace as a large leather watch case with a display top teetered on the arm of the big leather couch as a kid in a hoodie and a COVID mask was dodging Niven as she stood in front of the broken bay window swinging a fireplace poker in a vicious arc, blocking his exit as Jeep stepped in.

"GET ON THE FLOOR! NOW!"

The kid turned around, his hands out, eyes wide and pinned on the Glock leveled at his torso.

"NOW!"

"HE SAID NOW!" Niven roared, and then helped him along with a home-run swing to his left elbow. The kid howled and dropped and writhed. Jeep was on him in an instant, flipping him on his belly, gun to the back of his head, his free hand fast and rough in a frisk, then slapping the cuffs on and pushing off him and back on his feet.

He took it all in.

Jeep late to his calling. Check.

A woman he wanted and the man who broke into her home. Check.

Fire in the fireplace, so quick to an improvised weapon. Check.

Arbogast was right; irony finds you.

The kid complained in Spanish Jeep didn't understand.

"Give me a minute alone with him," Jeep said to Niven.

"For?" she said.

"Questioning."

She walked out and shut the door behind her.

"*¿Hablas inglés?*" Jeep asked.

"*No puedo,*" the kid said.

"You worthless fucking scumbag," Jeep said.

Jeep knew he had the right to teach the guy a lesson. A duty, even. A kick to his balls like a sixty-yard field goal attempt. A chit called in for all the ones who waltz away free.

Jeep flipped him on his back and grabbed a foot and hauled it out at a wide angle. The male swore at him in Spanish, trying to squirm away on the carpet.

Jeep looked at the kid and thought, his wrists must be killing him, all that weight and torque on the handcuffs biting into his flesh. Excellent.

Jeep froze. The room spun a little.

Jeep dropped the guy's foot.

He wasn't that cop and never would be. He wasn't the Avenger, and this kid wasn't the Martyr. Jeep was just a small-town cop and the boy was just another hapless loser.

The sirens of the Centre Brookville PD squads whooped their finale as they made the turn in and skidded to a stop.

Jeep sat down on the couch and checked out Niven's father's watch collection and waited for his officers.

Bondi secured the intruder in the back of Jeep's Tahoe while Jeep took down Niven's account in the living room as she sipped on a large bourbon and nibbled on a junior Valium.

Was reading her Kindle by the firelight (the new Erik Larson, highly recommended). Went to pee in back-hall half bath, came back to library to find her father's watch collection on the arm of the couch and the male pulling out desk drawers. Grabbed crystal globe from shelf by door (Dad's 2004 Brookside Club Men's Tennis Singles Champion trophy) and flung it but missed (always had a great arm "for a girl," but rusty) and broke window. Made quick fireplace-weapon connection, grabbed poker. Then you got here.

Jeep and Bondi ran the kid, one Lucas Alvarez of Santiago, Chile, over to the NCPD Second Precinct for processing. There was no desk appearance ticket bullshit this time; the kid, a stupidly greedy eighteen-year-old, was charged with multiple felonies and fed directly into the maw of the system. Which gave Jeep a warm and peaceful feeling, like a well-earned nightcap.

"What's with you and the widow Chambliss?" Bondi asked.

They were headed west on Jericho Turnpike, back to the crime scene for the wrap-up.

"Nothing."

"Something."

"I *said*, nothing. And she's not the 'widow Chambliss,' they divorced years ago."

"She remarry?"

"No."

"Then a distinction without a difference, where I come from."

"And where is that, exactly? Deadwood, 1880?"

Bondi would not be detoured.

"Watching you take her statement, there was an intimacy to it."

"We've known each other half our lives is all."

Bondi motored his seatback down some and pulled the visor of his cap over his eyes.

"Whatever you say, Chief."

Jackson and Diaz had sourced a tarp and ladders from the garage and covered up the broken panes in the bay window. It was Jeep's first stop when they got back to the scene.

"Nice work, you two. Going the extra mile," Jeep said, standing at the foot of Jackson's ladder.

"It's supposed to rain later so we thought to," Jackson said.

Jeep said, "Ms. Croft inside?"

"No, she asked did we need her or if she could head into the city, and we said no we didn't and yes she could, and an Uber came about a half hour ago, was that wrong should I have called you?"

"Not at all," Jeep said, as cool as he could.

Jeep stopped at Sid's in Glen Cove for a double cheeseburger and a can of Montauk Brewery IPA to go but ate the burger and drank the ale on the drive home. Eating alone late at night in front of the TV often left him blue and he didn't need any more reasons that night.

He pulled into his driveway just past ten thirty and of course there was no G-50 parked in its spot. The Mercedes had been stopped by an alert Jericho speed trap and was impounded as evidence and the thief had been booked. It was Cops 2–Robbers 0 for the night, silver linings–wise.

Jeep got out of the Tahoe and noticed the dimmest light through the picture window of the living room, glowing soft white, propped on a couch pillow. A Kindle.

Niven opened the front door.

"Hi," she said.

"They said you went to the city," he said.

"I changed my mind, obviously."

"What if I was with somebody, you ever think of that?"

"Of course I have," she said sincerely. "*Are* you expecting someone?"

He didn't answer that, just walked past her into the kitchen and tossed the Sid's bag and got another beer.

"I didn't want to be alone, all right?" Niven said.

"No worries," he managed, and popped the top. "You want a beer?"

She didn't answer. He walked back into the living room. She took a couple steps toward him, hesitant, for her. She took his beer and took a swallow and put it aside and took a step closer and looked him in the eye.

"Let's just get this over with, shall we?"

She pressed her mouth to his and found his tongue with hers. They danced like that for a while, swaying in his living room, kissing. Then with more urgency; their hands all over each other, rubbing, pinching, testing. Jeep found the waistband of her jeans and she sucked her tummy in. He slid his hand down and palmed the mound over the thin fabric of her underpants and pressed his middle finger in the crease there. He undid the button, pulled down the zipper, slid his thumbs in the elastic and shoved the whole deal down to her knees and broke the kiss.

"C'mon, say it."

"Say what," she managed, her breath coming fast.

"You know."

"I *don't*."

"What I said *you* said, that time."

"Oh . . . *oh.*"

She looked at him with the usual mischief but also some surrender.

"Feel how wet I am."

That early Sunday morning the beaches in Bayville were shared by the shorebirds grazing at the tidal buffet and the scatter of men and boys casting for porgies and sea bass. In the mile or so Jeep had walked before he had turned back for home the score was Shorebirds 9–People 1; a kid reeling in a bunker finally getting his team on the board and an osprey dive-bombing for a striper the likely Play of the Game.

If Jeep was a cartoon character, and this morning he certainly felt like one, he was Wile E. Coyote or Tom the Cat after being flattened by an Acme anvil or a felled tree in that sequence where they spend a few moments as staggering accordion versions of themselves before springing back to normal.

It wasn't just the night with Niven, though that was one for the ages, not least because of all the complicated ages that led up to it. It was also this place. On a map of the world, this little string of villages on the North Shore of Long Island measured a few square miles on a planet with almost two hundred million of them. On a map of Jeep's life, it could feel like they were the beginnings and the ends of the earth.

On this morning he was walking the exact stretch of shoreline where his dad had taught him to fish and to swim as a boy and talked him through the important stuff as a young man and still walked with Jeep in all the years since he was gone. On this stretch of shoreline Jeep's oldest friend had saved his son's life and lost his own in a collision between the past and the present. Here the past was always clawing or shoving at the present, like the tide dragging the shells and the driftwood into the sea and then tumbling it all back onshore, day in and day out.

But just up ahead the past was standing side by side with the present, on the bulkhead in back of the house he'd grown up in and still called home. She was fresh from his bed, wearing his old flannel robe and waving to him.

Jeep waved back and opened his arms to her, to all of it, to this place, in this minute, on this day and date.

Acknowledgments

This book was written during the long writers' and actors' strikes of 2023, which suspended all work writing for television and movies, the only job I'd had for a long time. One early Saturday morning a couple of months into the strike, my wife, Sasha, came into the kitchen to find me assembling the ingredients for a skillet cornbread recipe. I am not, by nature or custom, a baker. She took in the scene and said, "You need something to do," which resulted in the novel you just read.

For that, and for a lot of other good reasons, this book is dedicated to her.

Thanks also to our son, Luke, for his help with the research and his informed and unique point of view, and to our daughter, Maria, who was among the first readers and has been my sounding board for three decades now.

Early on I invited my friend, the renowned literary agent Esther Newberg, to lunch. I pitched her the rough story, the characters, and the title. She was encouraging in her famously pragmatic and wise ways. I can't thank her enough.

Esther gave some early chapters to Deb Futter, who offered to publish it. She was already enormously accomplished as an editor and publisher, and on that day she also became my new best friend.

It turns out you can have a whole career writing for the screen without ever once being checked for grammar, usage, and punctuation. This epic task fell to the editor Elizabeth Catalano, and I am grateful for her patience, kindness and wit in the manuscript margins, where I could not see her eyes roll.

Dan Norton has been my agent for many years, and his wise counsel has been as invaluable as his business smarts and enthusiastic support.

Thanks and owe-you-ones to Brookville Chief of Police Kenneth Lack, Nassau County Police Department Detective Mike Bitsko, Nassau County Police Commissioner Patrick Ryder, Manhattan DA's office Chief ADA Nicole Blumberg, and estates attorney John J. Randall IV for their invaluable guidance and expertise.

Over fourteen years, a small group of colleagues and I wrote and produced two hundred and ninety-three episodes of the CBS police procedural / family drama *Blue Bloods*. The dynamics of that mashed-up genre also drive this novel, and that recipe was tested and refined along with Brian Burns, Siobhan Byrne O'Connor, Ian Biederman, Dan Truly, Peter Blauner, Willie Reale and the other talented writers who joined for a spell along the way. Most especially, my respect, admiration and appreciation goes out to Siobhan, my better half on that job, who made the hard days easier with her grace, patience, and humor.

Retired NYPD Detective James Nuciforo was the technical adviser for the run of *Blue Bloods*, as well as for this book. I'm grateful for his expertise and friendship but also for his unique gifts as a storyteller, many of which I've stolen for use here.

About the Author

Kevin Wade is a playwright, screenwriter, and television writer and producer whose credits include the stage plays *Key Exchange*, *Mr. & Mrs.*, and *Cruise Control*, and the screenplays for *Working Girl* (seven Academy Award nominations), *True Colors*, *Mr. Baseball*, *Junior*, *Meet Joe Black*, and *Maid in Manhattan*. For television, he created the ABC drama *Cashmere Mafia* and in 2010 joined the rookie CBS drama *Blue Bloods* as a writer. Starting with the second season and for the rest of the show's fourteen-year run, Wade served as its showrunner, executive producer, and back-seat driver.

CELADON
BOOKS

Founded in 2017, Celadon Books, a division of
Macmillan Publishers, publishes a highly curated list
of twenty to twenty-five new titles a year. The list of
both fiction and nonfiction is eclectic and focuses
on publishing commercial and literary books and
discovering and nurturing talent.